I0587034

SURRENDER
TO THE
DUKE

Copyright

This book is a work of fiction. The names, characters, places, and incidents are products of the writer's imagination or have been used fictitiously and are not to be construed as real. Any resemblance to persons, living or dead, actual events, locales or organizations is entirely coincidental.

SURRENDER TO THE DUKE, The Wayward Woodvilles, Book 6 © 2022 by Tamara Gill
Cover Art by Wicked Smart Designs
Editor Grace Bradley Editing, LLC

ISBN: 978-0-6457257-6-6 (trade paperback)

ONE

"Harlow? What are you doing home?" Lila asked her sister as she strode into the front parlor of their modest country home, valise in one hand and pelisse in the other. Two footmen followed, carrying a large trunk upstairs.

"I've left London. The Season was too hectic, even for me, and I find it no longer holds my attention, so I wanted to come home and visit Mama and Papa." Harlow dropped her valise at her feet, the heavy bag making Lila start. "How are they, Lila? Has their health improved?" her sister asked, glancing up toward the first floor as if that would give her more insight.

"They are much improved and will soon be well enough to leave their room. I should think in the next week or so they'll return to their normal duties," Lila said, sitting back on the settee and picking up the knitting she was working on before her sister's arrival home. "I'm hoping Father will be well enough to look at the ledgers. The accounts are piling up, too much for even me to keep abreast."

"That is concerning, but very good about their health." Harlow came and sat across from her, slumping inelegantly on the settee, staring at the unlit hearth. "You must go to London, take my place in society, and finish the Season for me," she blurted, matter-of-fact.

"Me?" Lila stared at her. Had her sister lost her mind? "What do you mean to go to London and finish the Season for you?"

"Well," Harlow hedged. "Travel to town and pretend that you're me. We're the same height and wear the same size dresses, shoes, and gloves, and we are always getting muddled here in Grafton as to which one we are. You could return, and no one would be the wiser."

"But I do not want another Season. I had two, and they were all disasters. I was not as elegant as you, and they would see through my facade straightaway." She shook her head, the idea enough to make her head spin. "You are so silly to even think of such a plan."

Her sister sighed, slapping the settee cushion with her gloved hands. "You must return and let

Lord Billington down gracefully for me, for I did not have the heart to do so."

"Lord Billington is after your hand?"' Lila dropped her knitting, her sister gaining her full attention. She had met his lordship at her best friend and now the Duchess of Derby's wedding several years ago. He was a handsome man, kind and honest. She doubted many did not want to marry a man like his lordship.

Well, she had met him and had fallen spontaneously in love. Not that he even knew she breathed air on this world. The thought of his affections directed at Harlow twisted pain deep inside her, and she cringed. "Whyever do you not wish for Lord Billington's affections?" she asked, not quite sure she wanted to know. Not if she were to hear they merely had a disagreement and would soon be at rights again.

Her sister huffed out an annoyed breath and glared at her. "There are many gentlemen who have courted me this Season, and they are all very polite and what one may want in a husband, but I do not feel anything for Lord Billington. He does not make my heart race as it should. But I also cannot be cruel. Lord Billington, I believe, is on the cusp of asking for my hand, and I will feel so flawed to let him down."

Lila gaped at Harlow, not quite believing her sister's reasoning for this absurd plan. "And so you'll have me return to town, pretend I am you to let him down gently. You know I'm not capable of pretending anything. I'm a terrible actress, and you're much more delicate and ladylike than me. It is one of the reasons why your Season has been a success and mine have been two utter failures."

Her sister pushed up from the settee, coming to kneel before her. "Lila, please help me. I do not want to return to London. And if we set your hair just as I have mine, and you wear my gowns, no one will be the wiser. Everyone says we look like twins here in Grafton and Lord Billington, as much as he pretends to be interested in me, is only so because I'm the diamond of the Season. He will never know the difference."

"You forget that Hailey is in town, and she will see through my ruse and call me out on this flawed plan."

Lila shook her head, grinning. "Ah, but I have thought of that too. You must ask Her Grace to go along with our plan."

"Our plan. Your plan, you mean," she corrected.

"Fine." Her sister rolled her eyes. "My plan. And ask her to keep your secret for just the last few weeks of the Season. When you explain the reasons why she will understand."

Lila raised her brows. "No, she will not. She will think it as bad as I do. I will not involve her grace."

Harlow waved her concerns aside. "And you never know, Lila, maybe your time in London will be fruitful."

"Or I could be exposed as the fraud that I am to play and be ruined, and you along with me. Have you thought about that? People will think us a terrible family should they ever find out we played them all for fools."

Harlow took her hands, holding them tight. "Please, Lila. I cannot face Billington. I want to remain here with Mama and Papa. I want one more Season before I choose whom I will marry."

"Is there a reason you do not wish for Billington's suit? Has he been forceful or overstepped polite boundaries? What is troubling you really, Harlow?" Lila asked. There had to be more behind her sister's hasty removal from town. But what?

Her sister chewed her bottom lip, unable to meet her eye. "I love another, and he does not know that I even exist, but I will not marry merely anyone to secure a match. I will be a wallflower and old maid if I have to, so long as I do not make the disastrous mistake of marrying the wrong man."

Tears pooled in her sister's eyes, and Lila patted her hand, hating to see her upset. "Very well, I will go to town and make things right with Billington. We shall sort out the dresses tonight, and you will give me any outstanding invitations you have received. I will return to town for the next several weeks and settle everything amicably, so there is no ill will between Billington and yourself."

"You will?" Her sister met her eyes, hope drying up her tears. "Thank you so much, Lila. You are the best sister anyone could ever ask for. I do not know how to thank you."

Harlow sat beside her and pulled her into a fierce hug. "No one will know that you're not me. We even have the same freckle on our lip."

"Except on opposite sides of our mouths, Harlow," Lila mentioned.

Harlow waved her concerns aside. "No one will remember such a minor detail. All will be well, and you'll soon be home, and I shall prepare for next year's Season where I am determined to make Lord Kemsley see me this time, not ignore me as he has been doing. Frightful man."

"Maybe he is not the man for you. He should see you already, try to court you now if he has any interest. How could he not when you're so lovely and eligible?"

"Yes, but we're gentry, not nobility. Even our friends, the Woodvilles, have a little nobility in their bloodline, but we do not. All I have is my inheritance, same as yours, but that was not enough to garner you any offers."

Her sister's words cut a wound that had never healed. Her Seasons had been days and nights of nothing spectacular at all. How she had longed to be a success. To return home and declare to her family she had made a grand match. She had been a failure and not much else. "Except Lord Billington did not seem to mind such truths. Are you sure you wish to cut him free of your ties?" Lila asked again. As much as she admired Billington, he had not courted her when she was in London, and she could not stand in the way of her sister's happiness, not if Billington was whom she wanted and this whole game was a ploy to get him to fall even further in love with her.

"I do not want him as my husband. He is handsome, rich, everything a woman would want in a husband, but I do not get butterflies in my stomach when I look at him. In fact, I may as well be looking at a brick wall for all the emotion I feel. I may even feel more for the wall than I do his lordship."

Lila rolled her eyes, shaking her head at her sister's words. "You have made yourself clear. I will return to London tomorrow to save your hide. But this is the last time, Harlow. The next time a gentleman shows interest in you, and you do not have the heart to let him down nicely, neither will I. You will have to do it yourself or forever remain in hiding. Are we understood?" Lila stated, her words brooking no argument.

"I understand, and I concur. But you will see,

Lila. There will not be another such situation. The next time I'm in London, I will win Lord Kemsley's heart and have all I want."

"Let us hope that is so," Lila declared.

Her sister stood and flounced toward the stairs. "I will go and see Mama and Papa now and have your maid prepare your bags." Harlow stopped on the first step of the stairs, her visage serious all of a sudden. "I do appreciate this, Lila. You are the best of sisters."

Lila slumped back on the settee, not feeling like the best of sisters. She already felt like a liar, an imposter who had to notify an upstanding, genuine gentleman she did not want to marry him. The things she did for her sister. Never again. This would be the last time.

Two

Lila settled herself in the house her great aunt and companion for Harlow had leased for the duration of the Season. She sat on the settee in her room while her maid unpacked dresses, shoes, hats, and gloves, which she had packed up for Harlow only days before. The poor woman probably thought them both muddle-headed.

"Here you are, my dear. I'm so glad you changed your mind and returned to London," Aunt Mavis declared from the door before walking into the room and advising the maid on how to fold unmentionables. Her aunt was middle-aged with a full head of gray hair. She was her father's oldest sibling and stooped a little when she walked but still held the *joie de vivre* of a debutante enjoying her first steps in town.

"Thank you, Aunt. I'm delighted to be back. I thought over why I needed to depart, and it was only right that I return and finish the Season as I should. I hope you're not angry with me."

"Well," her aunt said, her mouth thinning into a displeased line. "Only a little dissatisfied, but should you make a grand match, I shall forgive all soon enough." The older woman chuckled and mumbled something about tea before wandering out the door without a backward glance.

Lila thumbed through the many event invitations Harlow had received. Many more than she had obtained when she was in London last. She wasn't fooled enough not to know why her sister was so favored among the fashionable *ton*. She was charismatic, amusing, and confident. So very different from herself when she was among large crowds. She was only ever comfortable around friends and family, but when among those she hardly knew, she always managed to have two left feet and a mouth that mumbled. Or at least it certainly felt as though that was so.

Lila took a calming breath. The thought of reentering society without her good friend Hailey beside her made her stomach churn. She would need to keep away from the duchess, for she knew as well as her parents how to decipher the differences between herself and Harlow. And the duchess would ask what she was about pretending to be her sister.

Not that she intended to be in London long enough to be caught. She would have an audience with Lord Billington, let him down in the kindest, quickest way imaginable, and be gone from London back to Grafton.

"Miss York, would you like to wear the lavender gown this evening?" her maid Jane said, holding up the pretty muslin gown that sported fuchsia flowers embroidered on the bodice.

"Yes, thank you," she said, flipping to the invitation she was to attend this evening. Lord and Lady Maddigon were an older couple in society but affable, she supposed. With any serendipity, the Woodvilles would be busy at other events and would not be present to try to out her duplicity.

"I will go downstairs and press the gown, Miss York. It is a little crinkled from your travels," Jane said, bustling out of the room and leaving her blissfully alone.

She supposed over the past few years, she had become quite accustomed to being alone and only attending the few events held at Grafton.

No one paid her any mind or cared that she was now firmly on the shelf. In truth, neither she nor her sister required marriage due to their large dowries, and Lila couldn't help but be a little pleased that one day she would answer to no one but herself.

Once upon a time, she would have loved a husband and children, but those dreams were gone now. She had just turned six and twenty, an old maid by society standards. Pretending to be her younger sister would require early nights and rest through the day.

She rolled her eyes. Wondered for the hundredth time since leaving Grafton why she had agreed to such a ridiculous plan.

Because you love your sister, that is why.

Lila pursed her lips, not entirely sure that would be the case after the next few weeks.

Knox King, Viscount Billington, stood before his looking glass, pleased with his valet's perfectly configured cravat tying. The man was a genius and well worth stealing from his good friend, the Duke of Renford.

"Thank you, Craig. That'll be all."

"Yes, my lord," his valet said, disappearing into his closet to no doubt tidy up the mess made by preparing for this evening's ball.

Excitement thrummed in his veins and, taking one last look at himself, he left the room. Tonight he would ask the delightful Miss Harlow York to be his wife. His future viscountess and eventual duchess when he came into the Lancaster title.

Picking up his hat and gloves from the chair

beside the door, he left his chamber and made his way to the waiting carriage. It did not take long to arrive at Lord and Lady Maddigon's London home, and he was pleased that the ball was already in full swing.

He made his way through the throng of guests, greeting those he knew and smiling at several young ladies who simpered in his presence. But he wasn't interested in them. He sought only one lady this evening.

The hairs on the back of his neck prickled, and he turned, a smile lifting his lips at the sight of Miss York, standing alone beside the ballroom floor, a glass of champagne in her hand.

She was a beautiful woman and would complement him and his name well. Although she came from humble beginnings, that did not matter much, not when she was the diamond of the Season and one of the wealthiest debutantes in town.

He started toward her, wanting to press his suit to see if she would be amenable to an offer of marriage.

Her timid smile caught him unawares as he bowed before her, taking her gloved hand and kissing it. "Miss York, it is good to see you again. We missed you at the Frost ball," he stated. "I hope you were not taken ill to remove you from our set those few days," he said, coming to stand beside her.

She bit her lip, and he studied her, wondering why she was so nervous about him. Miss York had always been quite the opposite, outgoing and opinionated, just the perfect temperament to handle the duties of a viscount and future duke. Even if most of that time, she also appeared uninterested and distracted.

She cleared her throat, refusing to do anything more than glance at him sporadically. "I'm very well, my lord. I merely wished for some time away, that is all," she said. "The Season can be so hectic."

He looked about the room, understanding her wish for some peace. The Season was often frenzied and constant, and it was not surprising she wanted a little respite. "Where is your good friend Viscountess Leigh? You are often never far from her." He took two fresh glasses of champagne from a passing footman and handed her one.

Miss York took a healthy sip before following that with another. "Ah, I have not seen her this evening, but I'm sure I shall," she said. "Are you enjoying the ball, my lord?"

He smiled at her. The deep-purple tone of her gown made her eyes a vibrant shade of green. The pit of his stomach clenched, and hope flittered through him that his choice of bride was satisfactory. He had been worried the chemistry he felt for Miss York was lackluster at best. Yes, she ticked all his boxes of what type of woman he ought to marry, but this evening, after having been away from Miss York for several days, he knew he was making the right decision. She was more beautiful this evening than he had ever seen her before, but there was something different about her he could not place. Not that it mattered. His gut told him his choice was correct, which counted most.

"I am, Miss York. All the more knowing that you are here." He sipped his champagne, giving himself courage. He'd never proposed to anyone before, which was not as simple as he first thought. "I was hoping to steal you away, to speak to you if you're willing. The terrace doors are open, and we will not be entirely alone."

Her eyes widened at his request, and after the many weeks of his courtship, she would be foolish if she did not have some inkling of what he was about to ask.

She took a fortifying breath and downed the last of her champagne. "Of course, my lord. A little turn on the terrace would be refreshing indeed," she said.

He held out his arm and she settled her hand upon it, then he escorted her outside. The warm evening air was refreshing after the stifling ball, and he led her along the terrace a little, giving them some privacy.

"I should imagine you're not so blind to know why I wished to speak to you."

"My lord, before another word is spoken—"

"That is to say, you must know how much I admire and like you, Miss York."

She bit her lip, something she had never done before, and the sight of her pretty lip held between her teeth made heat lick at his skin. He rolled his shoulders, his coat and cravat all of a sudden too stifling to wear. He rubbed a hand over his brow. Was he sweating?

"Of course, my lord, but—"

"And it is because of those emotions," he said, "that I must do the right thing as a gentleman and ask you, Miss York, to be my wife." He smiled, relieved to have finally spoken the words necessary for their courtship to come to a satisfactory end. "Will you marry me?"

THREE

N ow was the time to tell him. To let him know that her sister did not want to marry him, but the words would not form on her tongue. Instead, she stared at him, probably resembling a deer caught between two predators and not knowing which way to run to escape.

She clasped her hands in front of her, hoping her voice didn't tremble as she feared it would. She had never received an offer of marriage, even if this one wasn't hers. Still, it left her feeling all at odds and not at all comfortable.

"My lord, thank you for your kind offer," she said, meeting his eyes and hoping the expectation on his face did not mean he thought Harlow would agree to the marriage. They had only known each other for weeks at best. No, they had met at a house party several years ago, so they were not-too-recent friends. But still, there had been little contact after the Duke and Duchess of Derby's wedding. As Harlow had stated herself, he was only interested now because her sister had been named the diamond of the Season.

She shook the thought aside, concentrating on the assignment at hand. "Truly, it is a great honor to receive an offer from you, but I'm not certain that we're compatible," she said.

He raised his brows, a small smile twisting up his lips that did not quite reach his eyes. Oh dear, he was disappointed in the answer. She hated to make anyone upset, and she had always been too quick to please others. Hence, why she was here in the first place, letting a lord of the realm down adequately because her sister could not.

"I do not know what to say, Miss York. I thought your feelings were engaged."

"Oh, but they are," she blurted before she could wrench them back. *Stop this, Lila! You're making this whole situation even worse.* "I do like you, my lord. I merely wish to have my Season without the complications of being betrothed to you or anyone."

"Ah," he said, his smile more genuine. "You need time. Well that, Miss York, I can give you if that is what you wish. I will not push you, of course. I would never want to make you do anything you did not want. But may I defer until the end of the Season for a response from you? After you have the time you desire?" he asked.

He asked so sweet and politely that Lila found herself nodding, not knowing what else she could do. She could not state that it wasn't time that she needed after all, but that her sister did not want to marry him and was too much of a coward to tell him to his face. There were only a few weeks left of the Season. It would not be so hard to keep her distance and remain aloof. He would soon lose interest and look elsewhere for a wife. And then, before she returned to Grafton, she would explain again that she did not want to marry him, or at least her sister did not, and go home.

What a mess!

"Thank you, my lord, that is very kind of you, but what if you find another you wish to marry? Maybe you should not wait for me, as fickle of mind as I am." Lila cringed at her words, knowing she had made her sister sound flippant and not at all loyal.

He took in her words a moment, and her heart hurt for him. After all his careful and devoted words, did he suspect Harlow did not feel the same and was merely grasping the last small thread to give him hope?

The idea hurt her heart since she had always carried a little infatuation for the gentleman.

Lila took in his features. She had not seen him for several years, not since her friend's wedding, and he was as handsome as she remembered. Not that she thought he would remember her at all. Even when she was in town, she failed to catch the attention of any eligible man. That had not changed in all the years she had remained in Grafton.

Even if her friend Hailey invited her to London each year, she had refused. She did not want to look more desperate than she was already deemed merely by her age alone.

She inwardly sighed. How she would have loved Lord Billington to turn his attentions toward her. He was handsome, lean, broad-shouldered, and had a jaw cut from stone, she was certain. No, handsome was too benign a word to term him. He was utterly devastating to the eye, and that Harlow had caught that gaze, well, she could not help but wonder what was wrong with her sister that she did not fall at his feet like every woman in the *ton* had been trying to do for years.

The man her sister loved must be a Greek god if she would turn down Billington.

"I'm a patient man, Miss York, and after all, it will give me more time to change your mind." His wicked grin made heat kiss her cheeks, and she inwardly cringed when she let out a small giggle.

He is not saying these things to you, Lila, but to Harlow. Remember that, you dolt.

"Come, we shall return inside, and I will leave you to enjoy your evening, but for this night only. I have until the end of the Season to ensure your mind is clear and you know what you want. Namely me," he said, wiggling his brows.

Lila chuckled, taking his arm and letting him lead her back indoors. Her pleasure was short-lived when the Duchess of Derby strolled up to them, her smile forced and a contemplative light in her eyes.

"Lila, how very good to see you," she said, kissing her cheek. "I have missed you this Season. Is Harlow coming back to town soon? I would like to see her finish out the Season."

Lila fumbled to reply and looked to Lord Billington who appeared as confused as she was panicked. She cleared her throat and forced a smile on her lips. "You are mistaken, Your Grace. I am Harlow. Lila is back in Grafton, but I shall write, and convey to her your demand. I'm certain she will act and come to see you soon."

"Oh, I thought," the duchess hesitated. "Well, forgive me for confusing you with your sister. Even so, if I know Lila well, and I know her *very* well," the duchess stated, smiling up to Lord Billington. "She will not heed my request and will remain in the country."

"That is probably true, Your Grace," Lila answered.

"Lord Billington, it is good to see you again, but if you'll excuse me, I must speak to Miss York alone. Much to discuss, you understand," she said.

Lord Billington bowed to them both, an understanding smile on his mouth. "Of course. Until tomorrow, Miss York, I bid you a good evening."

Lila dipped into a curtsy. "Good evening, my lord." No sooner was she standing again had the duchess wrenched her to the side of the room away from the surrounding *ton*.

"I know it's you, Lila, what are you doing here pretending to be Harlow? I knew that you were not your sister when I saw you with his lordship. What has she managed to navigate you into?" she demanded, her words severe, and yet, scrutinizing the duchess, anyone watching them would assume they were speaking of pretty things like gowns and fragrant gardens.

Lila sighed, not quite believing she was here doing what she was either. She explained to Hailey the plan and how it had already gone astray. The duchess stared at her, mute for the first time in all the years she had known her, and dread balled in her stomach.

"Please tell me this is not what you have done. What if Billington finds out about this trickery? He'll be devastated and made to feel a fool. I do not like this plan at all."

"Well, neither do I, but Harlow was insistent that she could not let him down herself. She stated he was kind, even if a little aloof, and that to tell him no was beyond her capability. So I'm doing the deed instead, as silly and awful as that may sound."

"It's very foolish." The duchess's lips thinned into a displeased line. "If she is old enough to have a Season, she is old enough to let a gentleman down when he asks for her hand, and the feelings are not reciprocated."

"I know." Lila sighed again. "I tried to persuade her otherwise, but no matter what she said to Billington to dissuade him, nothing worked. I'm the last resort."

"You need to tell him soon that his suit is not wanted."

"I tried," she said, a little too loudly, catching other guests' attention. "But he did not listen to me. He took my words as a means to give him another several weeks before he would ask again. He thinks to change my mind."

The duchess's brows rose, and a small, amused smile crossed her lips. "What if he tries to seduce you to his charms? Do you know if your sister has ever kissed his lordship?"

"I do not believe so. She is not romantically interested in his lordship and deep down she does not think he is interested in her either. Not really. That he is merely bedazzled a little by her being the diamond of the Season. Harlow is keen on

Lord Kemsley and hopes for a courtship with him next Season."

"Hmm, well, let us hope you are right, but Billington is a man, and a very handsome, virile one. What if he does try to kiss you? Whatever will you do?"

"I will not kiss him back," she stated. The thought of doing such a thing was beyond comprehension. She had never kissed a man in her life, even if the one man she had only ever wondered about had been Billington. But that was only because he was one of the first titled gentlemen she had met at Hailey's wedding. No doubt, a little of her infatuation resulted from her being awestruck by his grandeur and his looks.

He was devastatingly handsome, after all.

"It is not so easy as that, my friend. Some men are hard to resist. I know that better than anyone." Hailey cast a look toward the duke, who met his wife's eyes across the ballroom floor, a knowing smile passing between them.

That look—devotion, and love wrapped so tightly together that the bond was unbreakable—was what she wanted too. When they had married, her heart had stirred, and she knew she would never settle for less than what her friend had. In her Seasons in town, no one had ever tried to get to know her, win her heart for themselves. Not even Billington, who at that time was more rake and rogue than a man trying to find a wife.

But this year, it seemed his mind had changed. Why had she not come to town with her sister? Maybe he would have turned his attention to her instead of Harlow. Maybe even now, she would have been engaged to the man of her dreams.

Fanciful, but still what she would have loved had it come to fruition. "Do not be concerned with that, Hailey. I will not be doing anything that will prolong this agony."

"I cannot believe either of you thought this was a good idea."

"I did not," she defended. "I tried to talk her into returning and doing all of this herself, but she flatly refused. I did not think anyone would recognize me. I'm only here to end the Season and hoped to avoid you."

"Yes, I can see that because you know I would pick you out of a thousand Harlows, and I did. You realize you have a mole above each of your lips on different sides of your face, do you not?"

"We're not twins," she argued. "And yes, I'm aware."

"But you look like twins, and Billington has no idea." Hailey shook her head, a frown between her brows. "I do not like this idea, Lila, and I fear this will not end well."

Lila groaned. "You are not the only one."

Four

The following morning Lila sat in the drawing room at her aunt's London home, flipping through the pages of the latest *La Belle Assemblée*. Her aunt sat before the fire, something she always had burning no matter how warm the days were in London.

Today was no exception. Lila had set herself as far away from the heat as possible, but still, she felt the prickling on her skin and the small sheen of sweat in the stifling room.

A knock on the door sounded, and her aunt bade the servant entry.

"A Lord Billington to see Miss York," he stated, waiting at the door for a reply.

Lila looked to her aunt, whose large smile told her all she needed to know about her aunt's thoughts of Harlow being courted by the viscount.

"Oh well, send him in, James. We are at home

for such visitors," her aunt said, patting her hair and putting away her knitting.

Lila stood when Lord Billington strode into the room. She pushed down the nerves and butterflies she felt every time she was in his presence. He was so tall, stately, and seemed to vaporize all the air in the room, leaving her breathless.

"Mrs. Chapman, Miss York, I hope you do not mind my calling on you without an invitation, but the day is very fine, and I thought Miss York might like a drive about Hyde Park," he offered. His smile, which always affected the ladies of the *ton*, seemed to function well on her aunt too, and a light, rose blush spread across her cheeks.

"I'm certain Harlow would like that very much, Lord Billington. You may take my maid, Harlow, as chaperone," she said.

Lila knew there was little she could do to get herself out of this situation, and so she did what every young lady in her position would do. She looked pleased about the outing, even if it weren't truly meant for her.

Maybe the opportunity to tell him that she did not wish to marry him would arise again, and he would believe her this time.

"I will go fetch my bonnet, my lord and meet you on the front steps, if that is agreeable?" she asked him.

He nodded. "Of course."

Lila slipped past him, ignoring the lump of nerves in her stomach. He smelled divine today, sandalwood, a raw and earthy scent she had always coveted. Did he wash with soap of the same scent, or did he use some lotion after bathing?

The idea of him lathering his skin, running his large hands over his muscular form made her knees tremble.

How was she to stop acting like a besotted fool when it was not even her that Billington was interested in? He wanted to marry her sister, not herself.

She needed to remember that fact now more than ever.

A few minutes later, the maid following close on her heels, they left the house, the carriage waiting before the steps with two chestnut mares dozing in the afternoon sun. Lila took Billington's hand to step up into the carriage. His fingers were warm, and his thumb caressed the top of her hand through her gloves, making goosebumps rise on her skin.

Oh dear, her agreeing to help her sister was a foolish idea. How was she supposed to stop reacting to him when all she did was respond to his every word and touch?

Maybe she should flee to Grafton and let him come to their home where she could let her sister do what she should always have done in the first place.

With her maid seated behind her with a footman, Billington settled beside her and picked up the reins, urging the horses to move on.

"The streets are busy this afternoon. I suppose people are making the most of the warm weather we're enjoying today," Lila stated. She bit her bottom lip, hating that her conversation ideas were less than interesting. It was all her mind's fault. If she did not speak of the weather, she could be tempted to talk of how handsome his profile was or if she could feel his arm to prove to herself that it was as taut as she imagined.

Oh dear lord, she was a wanton.

This is what happens when a woman of six and twenty is left to rusticate out in the country for too many years.

"It is why I wanted to extract you from the indoors and enjoy an outing with you. A little time in the sun makes your cheeks a very becoming shade of pink." He grinned at her. "I noticed the last time we went on such a jaunt."

Lila met his eyes, hoping he did not ask her about their previous carriage ride about the park as Harlow had not told her of it, what they had seen, or to whom they had talked.

That he thought her pretty when blushing brought pleasure to her, even though she knew the compliment wasn't for her. Playing someone else's role was difficult, and she wasn't prepared for it. He would find her out, then hate her and Harlow forever.

The thought that she would hurt him was wretched, and she should tell him the truth now. Or at least demand that he listen to her answer to his marriage question and set him free.

"I do not deserve such compliments, my lord," she said instead. "Not after I failed to give you the answer you require. You ought to compliment other young ladies who do seek your favor." There, she had said again that she was not looking for a union with him, more forthright than she had at the ball last evening.

"*Yet*, Miss York. You do not seek my favor yet." He studied her a moment, and she could read the disappointment in his blue eyes. "I hope you're still willing to allow me to change your mind?" he asked, his tone sincere.

The concern she read in his eyes could not bring forth the words she ought to say to him. Instead, Lila found herself mumbling words she should never speak. "Of course, my lord. I have not gone back on our agreement," she said, settling against the leather seat as they turned into Hyde Park.

The park was a hive of activity. Couples and acquaintances strolled the paths, numerous carriages ran along the few drives available, and families picnicked under the trees, their laughter carrying across the grassy verges separating them.

"How pleasant Hyde Park is. I had forgotten how much I loved coming here during the Season."

Billington looked at her, his brow furrowed. "We drove in the park last week, Miss York. I fear my courting of you has been a tremendous failure if you cannot remember our outing."

The derision in his voice made her cringe. "Oh no, I enjoyed our carriage rides."

"Our one carriage ride, this is your second."

Lila swallowed the panic rising in her throat. She was making too many mistakes, and he would find her out. This was precisely why she did not want to pretend to be Harlow in the first place.

"We should go for a picnic, my lord. If the weather holds, tomorrow may suffice," she suggested, hoping they had not already been on one and recently.

She did not need to be corrected or looked at as if she had windmills in her head. That quota had more than been filled already.

BILLINGTON DID NOT KNOW WHAT WAS muddling Miss York today, but she seemed out of sorts, and not to mention forgetful. He would not have thought their outing in Hyde Park last week easy to overlook since he had tried and successfully failed to steal a kiss.

He frowned as they passed a line of carriages. He dipped his hat and greeted those who passed them, but kept up a steady clip of his two chestnut mares.

"A picnic we have not enjoyed, but that is a sound idea," he said, thinking of where they could go that was different from the park and less crowded. He needed to get her to feel something for him other than benign friendship. He may not love the chit, but she was the diamond of the Season, intelligent and wealthy. All things a man of his station wanted in a wife, or so he was led to believe. That she did not seem overly keen on his suit left him puzzled. But he would give it one last month in an attempt to win her affections before moving on.

"I will consider the matter and discuss the outing at this evening's ball if you like. Are you attending Lord and Lady Astor's outdoor ball? I understand her ladyship has set up the ballroom that it partially stretches over the large lake on their grounds."

"Really?" Miss York gasped. "I am to attend, but I did not know their property in London was so grand to have such a water feature," she said, her shock clear to hear in her voice.

"The home has been in the family for hundreds of years. They're one of the oldest families in London, and the estate here in town rivals Devonshire House."

"Gosh, well, I'm looking forward to seeing it." She met his eyes, and that feeling in the pit of his gut was back. A clench, a need that he had not felt before. Not before she had left London and then hastily returned.

Her departure must have shocked him out of his undecidedness and made him realize that she was the woman for him. A little distance was what he needed to come to realize that fact.

"Will you promise me the first two dances?" he asked.

A coy smile lifted her lips, and the urge to dip his head and steal a kiss was almost too much to deny. She was so utterly charming, not to mention beautiful, and since returning from Grafton, she was much calmer, more dignified, and pleasant.

What had happened to bring on such a change of character?

Not that he did not like Miss York before her leaving, but he had always felt that he was bothersome to her rather than not.

"I'm certain I can, my lord." Miss York lifted her face to the sun, a small breeze lifting a curl to tickle the underside of her chin.

"You seem to be enjoying the outdoors today, Miss York. I did not think you liked the possibility of freckles."

She opened her eyes, the edges crinkling with mirth. "I love the outdoors. If I said otherwise, I must have been mistaken," she said, throwing him a cheeky grin he had never seen before on her face. "Or a little out of sorts that day."

He chuckled. Her appearance left her looking young and alive, excited to be with him. The knowledge gave him hope, and the day became all the brighter for it.

FIVE

L ila knew she ought to pretend to be like Harlow, to disagree and not enjoy her outing with Lord Billington, but the day was too lovely to ignore, and she could never understand Harlow's aversion to summer.

"The Royal Academy of Art is holding its annual exhibition. It's been open since May, but I thought if you would like to attend, I'd be more than willing to escort you," Lord Billington asked her.

Lila met his gaze, having never been, not even when she was in London having her Seasons, but it was an exhibition she had always wanted to view. "I would love that, my lord. Thank you," she said, forgetting she was supposed to be spending less time with him, not more. "When would you like to go, before or after our picnic?"

"Before, if you're willing." He paused. "Would tomorrow be too soon?" He clipped the reins over the horses' rumps, and they increased their pace as they came full circle in the park and out near the gates.

"I have no fixed engagements tomorrow." Lila fought not to wiggle with excitement. She told herself it was not because she would get to spend more time with the lovely Lord Billington at her side, but because he was taking her to view art. Not that she could paint or draw particularly well, but that did not mean she did not appreciate it from those who could.

They made their way through Mayfair and toward Queen Street, and a comfortable silence settled between them. Every so often, the movement of the carriage would make their arms brush, and each time the pit of her stomach would clench. She needed to gain more control over the emotions that bombarded her whenever she was around him.

But it wasn't easy when he was so very sweet and accommodating. It was hard not to imagine him saying those things to her instead of her sister. To not fall under his roguish charm.

The carriage rolled to a stop before her aunt's home, and he jumped down, reaching up to assist her to alight. Instead of taking her hand, he clasped her about the waist and lifted her to the cobbled sidewalk as if she weighed nothing more than a feather.

Lila let out a little squeal, and heat kissed her

skin. His smile made the butterflies crash about inside her a second time before he lifted her hand and kissed her gloved fingers.

"Until tomorrow, Miss York," he said.

Lila nodded, taking back her hand before she did something foolish, like throwing herself at his feet like the loveless old maid she was. He climbed back into his carriage, and she enjoyed the view of him doing so, regardless of the pointed look her maid gave her at her ogling.

"Tomorrow, my lord." She waved him off before returning indoors. Tomorrow could not come soon enough.

LILA SLEPT VERY LITTLE DURING THE night. She tossed and turned, her excitement over her outing today making it impossible for her mind to rest.

She debated what gown she would wear and what bonnet. If she had matching gloves and whether to wear boots or slippers. Probably boots, since slippers were not made for prolonged walking on anything other than ballroom floors.

A note arrived just after breakfast that Lord Billington would come to collect her after lunch, and Lila fought to keep herself occupied before he arrived.

She sat in the drawing room, knitting a shawl for her mama for her upcoming birthday, and tried to ignore every carriage that rumbled by on the road.

"He'll be here soon enough, Harlow. Do not be so eager, or he may take advantage of your interest for his lordship," her aunt said, sipping her tea, the book in her lap forgotten while she studied Lila instead.

"I'm not eager to see Lord Billington, but the exhibition," she lied, hoping her aunt would stop leaping to conclusions that were not wholly incorrect. However, the thought of having his lordship all to herself for several hours did leave her all but bouncing in her chair with excitement.

"Whatever you say, dear," her aunt said, her tone one of disbelief.

A knock echoed throughout the foyer, and Lila stood, startling her aunt. Her knitting fell to the floor, and she quickly bent to pick it up and pack it away before the footman notified them of their visitor.

"Lord Billington is here for you, Miss York," James stated from the door.

"Off you go, my dear. Remember to take your maid and enjoy the art. I may drop in on the exhibition before it is over myself."

Lila kissed her aunt goodbye. "You should. It is supposed to be very good," she said.

"You'll be able to tell me soon enough when you return."

Lila followed the footman and found Lord

Billington cooling his heels in the foyer. He bowed, his smile lighting up the modest space and making her feel giddier than she already did.

"Miss York. I hope you're ready for our outing?" he asked, giving her his arm.

She entwined hers with his and allowed him to lead her toward the carriage, her maid following them close on their heels. "I'm more than ready. I had wanted to visit the exhibition when I was in town some years ago but never got—" Lila halted her words, hoping he was not listening as closely as she feared he was.

He helped her into the carriage and settled beside her, throwing her a muddled glance. "Several years ago? But is this not your first Season? I thought I would have remembered you," he said.

But he had not remembered her at all. At least not Lila. She had seen him in town during her two Seasons, and not once had he even glanced in her direction. The thought reduced a little of the pleasure of the outing.

"Before I was out and we were in town, but my parents refused to escort my sister and me," she fibbed, hoping he would forget her slip.

"Ah, yes, I remember your sister. Is she not married now? I thought I heard she was," he said.

Lila looked out onto the bustling streets, swallowing the lump in her throat, knowing that she was definitely not married or anywhere near becoming so. "No, she is not married. She had two Seasons in London and did not garner one offer. I suppose she is what you would term an old maid." Lila fought not to scream at the unfairness of it all. Of how men could be of any age and marry, and while she, merely six and twenty, was too long in the tooth for anything but chaperoning. Or assisting a younger sister who had found herself in a situation not of her liking.

"I do not believe it. I know she is a favorite of the Duchess of Derby. Surely you must be mistaken," he argued.

Lila scoffed. "I think I would know if my sister were married or not, my lord." No matter how hard she tried, she could not mask the disdain in her voice.

"I meant no disrespect. I merely remember her being as handsome as you, so I'm surprised she is not."

His compliment went a little ways in taking the sting out of the fact that she was still unmarried and had no children of her own. How she longed to be a mother, to run a household of her own and not merely help out at her parents' small estate.

"Flattery will get you nowhere," she quipped, more than ready to let the subject of herself go. "Tell me, my lord. Are you an enthusiast of art? Have you been to the exhibition before?"

The carriage turned down Piccadilly, the thoroughfare busier than she had ever seen it before. "I have in past years, but not this one. I think you shall enjoy it. There is always something interesting to study."

"I cannot paint or draw and do not play the pianoforte very well at all."

His chuckle caught her attention, and she looked at him. "What do you find amusing, my lord?" she asked.

"You play the pianoforte very well. I have heard you at several musical evenings. I think you're being too modest, Miss York."

Lila nodded, turning to look in the direction they were traveling. If she were not careful, he would become suspicious of her. Of course, Harlow could play the piano, her sister had been determined from an early age to be proficient, but Lila had not. While she liked listening to music, she had no desire to learn how to create it.

"I thank you for the compliment," she said instead, preferring to let him think she was too modest to admit to her greatness. Or at least her sister's greatness.

The carriage rolled to a halt before the Royal Academy, the viscount's footman jumping down to open the door and hold the horse's reins while they viewed the exhibition.

He did not attempt to lift her down today, playing the gentleman instead and holding out his hand, and she took it, welcoming the strength of his hold. She really ought to stop reacting to him so, an almost-near-impossible thing to do since he seemed to overawe her at every moment.

"Shall we?" he asked.

Lila took his arm as they moved through a large arch to where others strolled toward the doors of a building farther away. "We shall," she agreed.

Six

Knox took more delight in watching Miss York regard the art than he did viewing the art himself. She clutched at his arm when a painting took her attention. He could not say whether she knew or not that she had done so, but the wistful smiles and constant chatter regarding the art were indeed enjoyable.

The more time he spent with Miss York, the more he enjoyed her company. There had been a change in her since her return to London. A warmth that had not been there before, not for him in any case. He had expected her to deny him immediately upon his proposal, but she had not. She had gifted him until the end of the Season to change her mind, something he did not think she would do, even if he begged.

Her steps slowed before one painting in particular, and he stopped to inspect it also. A woman sitting alone in a room while knitting.

"You like this drawing?" he asked. "I will admit that the lady looks very relaxed and unpretentious in this sketch," he said.

Miss York sighed, nodding. "She does, doesn't she? I myself enjoy knitting. It settles me, and one can create many useful articles when one becomes proficient."

He smiled, glad he had learned at least one thing about her. She had been so closed off from him, keeping all her secrets locked away, that he feared he would never know the real Miss York who had won over society so well.

"I cannot knit myself, but then I have never tried. Perhaps one day you will teach me," he said.

She met his eyes, hers alight with pleasure. "You would truly wish for me to teach you, my lord?" she asked him, her tone one of uncertainty. She did not believe him, but he was honest in his wish to learn. If only to spend more time with her.

"Of course. We may start tomorrow if you like. If you think your aunt would not mind, maybe we could lunch together in the drawing room and start our lessons after that?"

Her small, uncertain smile made his gut clench. She was so beautiful, so unassuming of the power she held over those near her. She was the diamond of the Season, and yet the lady before him did not seem at all knowledgeable of the fact. She seemed unsure and doubtful of the hold she held on people.

Him most especially.

"You wish to call on me, have luncheon together and knit the afternoon away?" she asked, her brows raised in disbelief.

He reached out and took her hand, placing it back on his arm before moving on from the painting. "You enjoy the hobby and I want to spend time with you, prove that what you love I can love too, then yes, I would like you to teach me."

She studied him a moment, and he could read the disbelief in her eyes before she raised her chin, making her more adorable than he thought possible.

"Why do you wish to marry me? Truly? What attracted you to me first and made you decide that no one else would do as your wife?"

They strolled for a few steps as he gathered his thoughts. "You were honest, which is a rarity in this society. You were favored, yes, and sought after, but you were not lofty with this revelation. You did not lead gentlemen on whom you did not want courting you."

"Bar the exception of you," she stated, a small smile playing about her sweet mouth.

He chuckled. "Yes, bar the exception of me because I could not give you up so easily. You were kind and generous to ladies who did not have a large social set. You used your friendship with Viscountess Leigh to help them move into society without fear. I thought you kind."

"And honest?" She bit her lip, stopping to stare at a painting of children playing in a park.

"Yes, I pride myself on being honest. I have never tried to hide my past, which as a young man in society could be termed questionable at times, but I was young and not ready to settle down. Now that I am, I'm looking for a wife who will always tell me the truth no matter what. I think you are that lady. You proved that to me when I asked for your hand, and you shared that you thought we would not suit directly to my face. The *ton* is full of men and women who lie every day to gain what they want, and I promised myself I would never be like that, and nor are you, which," he said, wagging his brows at her, "makes you perfect for me."

LILA SWALLOWED THE TRUTH THAT SHE wanted to cast up all over the exhibition's polished floors. He thought her truthful. An honest woman? How wrong he was. Her sister had ensured she was far from, that she was the biggest liar in England. He ought to be told the truth, that she was not Harlow and that his sweet words had no effect on the lady he thought he was courting.

For her, however, the effect was devastating. She adored being seen and spoken to like an intelligent woman. That he cared enough to learn how to knit told her all she needed to know about him. He was doing all he could to make her change her mind, be interested, and engaged. How could Harlow not fall for such sweet gestures?

How was she ever to stop herself from wanting to hear more from him? Of being with him? How was she to stop herself from falling for his charms when she had no right to do so?

"I am not so perfect, my lord. You ought not to place me on such a high moral pedestal," she said, trying to dissuade him.

"I speak as I find, and you have been nothing but charming. How could I not say such things about your person?"

Lila turned her attention back to the paintings, needing the subject of her high morals to be long over. The guilt that prickled her soul was enough to buckle her knees. "Are there any paintings here that you like, my lord? You know what I do, but you have said very little yourself."

"Hmm," he murmured as they continued along the corridor, the numerous paintings hung there for their enjoyment staring back at them. "I like any paintings, really, but I suppose the landscapes are my favorite. I adore living in the country. Returning to Billington Estate when the

Season is over is one of my favorite times of the year." He gestured to a painting, the wild highland mountains in the background, gentlemen in the foreground, guns and dogs at their sides. "Grouse season especially. I have a small estate in Scotland that I travel to yearly to partake in the sport. Do you hunt, Miss York?" he asked her.

"Rarely," she answered. "I like foxes and could not hurt them. And while I've never been grouse hunting, I'm sure I probably would not care to see that sport either." She glanced at him, trying to gauge his reaction to her not particularly liking what he did for a hobby. "Does this make me a little less attractive in your eyes, my lord?" Please say that it did. She needed to do something to make him turn from his suit of her.

"Not at all. It merely tells me yet again you're not a woman who will deceive, even to make yourself more attractive to those seeking to win you."

Win her? The man was too devastatingly sweet for his own good. His gaze dipped to her lips and settled there, and need twisted in her stomach. Never had a man looked at her the way Lord Billington did, and it was both shocking and exciting in its entirety.

"You are very forward with your regard, Lord Billington. Surely you cannot be so set on me that I'm the only object of your charming words," she teased.

"You are the only woman I'm interested in, Miss York, as you well know."

Lila turned to face him and found herself all too close to his chest. The scent of sandalwood teased her senses, and she closed her eyes momentarily, reveling in the woody, earthy tones.

Blast it, he smelled divine. That his looks fell under that same description was not at all fair. Not when she was supposed to be dissuading him but was failing miserably at that.

"You need to stop saying such things before someone hears," she admonished.

A devilish grin lifted his lips, and never in her six and twenty years had she ever wondered what it would be like to kiss such wicked lips. Would he kiss her back? Would he scoop her into his arms and make her lose what little control she had left around his lordship?

He was so charming. How could one not fall under his spell?

"It is true, and there is no shame in that." His hand brushed a loose curl from her cheek, slipping it behind her ear. "I have several weeks to win you, Miss York. Today is merely the beginning of my charms. I have many more in store for you, not just in the next month, but for all our married lives."

"Such as?" she found herself asking, longing tearing through her like a sword, cutting away her defenses.

"More of my charming self, days and nights of fun and adventure." He stepped closer still, and she could feel the heat of his body against her chest. Her nipples hardened, and her breath hitched. "Pleasures of the flesh, day and night, kisses that will take your breath away and make your heart stop. I will give you everything I have to offer, Miss York, and more."

Lila found herself swaying toward him and his intoxicating charm. However would she deny herself a taste of such sweet bliss?

She was doomed to fail.

SEVEN

Lila had everything prepared the following afternoon for Lord Billington's arrival and a lesson in knitting. Her aunt had agreed to allow them to be alone, so long as the drawing room door remained open and a footman stood outside the entire time of his call.

Excitement thrummed through her as she checked the drawing room was as it should be. The cushions were plump, the tea hot, and freshly cut cucumber sandwiches sat ready for them to break their fast should he wish it, along with an assortment of her favorite cakes.

A knock sounded on the front door, and the steps of a footman soon sounded on the foyer floor before he entered the room. "Lord Billington is here to see you, Miss York."

She smiled at the servant, unable to remove the excitement she felt at seeing Lord Billington again. "Thank you, James. You may send him in," she said, clasping her hands at her front to stop their shaking.

Lord Billington strode into the room a moment later, tall and as handsome as she knew him to be. His dark hair looked windswept, and a light blush sat on his chiseled cheeks.

He bowed, coming over to take her hand. He met her eyes as his lips touched the top of her fingers, and heat pooled at her core. Oh dear lord, he was too much for her desperate heart to deny.

"Miss York. You look beautiful as usual," he said. He did not let go of her hand; instead, he pulled her closer still. She let out a little yelp before his lips touched her cheek, kissing her more intimately than she had ever been kissed by a man before in her life.

What would he do if she were to turn her head and place her lips but a breath from his?

Before she could think better of it, she did just that. Their breath mingled, hot and panting. His hands tightened against hers, and for one delicious, intoxicating moment, she thought he might break all etiquette and bestow upon her her first kiss.

His eyes darkened, and she could read the need that burned in his blue gaze. A need she, too, found increasingly harder to deny.

"Are you ready for your first lesson, my lord?" she whispered.

Her words went a little way in bringing them

back to what was proper and expected of them. He moved away, clearing his throat. "Of course." He glanced at the knitting she had set out on a table before the hearth and settees. "I see you are well prepared for our lesson today."

Lila chuckled, another trait of hers that her sister, unfortunately, did not share. Her organizational skills were legendary in her home in Grafton.

"Yes," she said. "Shall we begin?"

He nodded and waved her before him so she could take her seat. She sat beside him, needing to be near him to instruct him on his first knitting lesson.

She held up two long needles. "These are knitting needles, and they will be used to make up the stitches that knot together to make clothing, scarfs, hats, whatever your heart desires."

His small smile warmed her in places that no woman of breeding ought to feel warmth. Not one who was unmarried and a veritable spinster.

"I use wool from a sheep to knit, and I have some yarn here. What would you like to try first? Just some standard stitches to form a scarf, perhaps?" she asked him.

"I think that would be best," he said. "I do not think my abilities will extend to anything extravagant."

"It may one day. You will merely have to continue practicing."

"With you?" he asked, holding her attention and pinning her with eyes that flickered with heat and made her nervous.

"If you wish to practice until the end of the Season, that, of course, can be arranged. After that, I'm still undecided," she lied, knowing she could not marry him. Harlow would never forgive her if she said yes to his proposal, knowing it was not Harlow at all who was answering such a profound question.

"You, Miss York, are a hard nut to crack, but I'm enjoying the challenge."

"I'm not so much of a challenge, my lord," she said.

"Oh yes, you are, more than you give yourself credit for. And please," he continued. "Call me Knox, Lord Billington, or my lord is too formal for my liking. I want to hear my name on your lips."

Lila swallowed. He wanted to hear his name on her lips? What did that mean? Did she have the nerve to ask? "Why would you like to hear Knox stated from my lips?" It seemed she was bold enough to inquire.

She knotted the wool about his knitting needle, handing him them both so he could start.

"So I can imagine you are saying my name in other...situations," he suggested.

She bit her lip, nerves tingling down her spine. "Will you elaborate?"

He shook his head, moving his attention back to the needles. "I think I have been devilish enough already today. Maybe we ought to concentrate on my lesson before I try to teach you other things we can do when we're alone."

This conversation was too forward and enlightening for her to give it up so easily. Whether it was appropriate or not, she wanted to know what he was thinking. What did he want to do with her? What did his words mean?

"We are not allowed to do anything when we're alone, or my choice whether to marry you or not would not be mine anymore," she said. "That does not mean I'm not curious."

A muscle worked in his jaw, and he took a calming breath. "I would not force you, whether we did anything or not, but it does not change the fact that I want to kiss you so very badly that my body aches from the denial of it," he admitted, meeting her eyes across the settee.

HE SHOULD NOT HAVE SAID WHAT HE DID, nor would he deny what he felt for the woman beside him. She was unassuming, and that fact alone drove him to distraction. Not to mention her beauty outshone all others.

When had he become so infatuated with her?

He supposed it was when she returned from Grafton, a woman who knew what she wanted and was honest with her choices. Even if he was determined to change those choices and convince her otherwise.

She shuffled a little away from him, picking up her needles. "You thread the needle through this loop and wrap the yarn about the top of the needle like this," she said, changing the subject. "Then you bring the needle down through here, and you'll see the loop-remaining yarn on the other needle, and that's your first stitch," she said, showing him her little stitch.

He attempted what she taught him, resulting in nothing but the first loop on his needle and no stitch. She chuckled, gesturing for him to try again. "It will take time and practice, but I'm certain you'll soon learn."

"I have nimble fingers. I'm determined to master knitting if only to impress you." Knox tried again, this time succeeding in forming another stitch on his needle. He laughed, showing her, surprised at his own pride at having accomplished what she taught. "I did it. You're a good teacher, Miss York."

"Keep going," she urged him, see if you can finish the first line." She leaned over beside him, guiding him, her hands touching his, moving his fingers to support the stitches so he would not drop one. All the while, the scent of jasmine taunted his senses. Not to mention she bit her bottom lip when she concentrated, which made the blood in his veins burn hot.

"May I say something, Miss York? And it's something that may shock you."

She met his eyes, not moving away as she should. "What do you wish to say to me?" she asked him.

Knox settled the knitting on his lap, meeting her wide, curious eyes. "You have little idea, do you, what happens to me when you touch me as you have been. As innocent as guiding my hands to knit, your touch sparks a hunger in me that will not be doused. And I cannot help but wonder if you feel as I do."

Her mouth opened with a slight gasp, and he fought not to seize her mouth or kiss her until they both lost themselves in each other's arms. "I want you as my wife. I want you in my bed and beside me for the rest of my days. Tell me that I have some chance of winning your hand, for being with you, having you near me, and knowing that I may not win your affections is killing me inside," he admitted, having never been so truthful with a woman in his life. But also, never having felt the need to. But with Miss York, it was different. He was different.

"How is it that you can want someone so much? You barely know me, Knox," she said.

He closed his eyes, savoring the sound of his name on her lips. He liked hearing her say it just so, wanted to listen to her moan his name in the grips of pleasure. "I know what I want, and I want you." He played with her fingers, warm and soft. "You are different from the other ladies of the *ton*. There is no falseness to you. Not to mention you are intelligent and kind. You will make the perfect viscountess and future duchess, and I will make it my life's mission to ensure you enjoy every moment of your married life with me."

Her gaze dipped to his lips, and he closed the space between them, his lips brushing hers in excruciating temptation.

A throat cleared in the foyer, and he stilled. Lila let out a little yelp and jumped to her feet, the dark blush on her cheeks proof of his wrongdoing.

The light, airy voice of the Duchess of Derby sounded at his back. "Miss York, Lord Billington, how pleasant to see you today."

Knox stood and laid down his knitting on the small table before them. "Your Grace, it is very good to see you."

The duchess stared at him, her attention snapping between them both. "While I do not believe that for a moment, I will bid you good morning, Lord Billington. I have an engagement with Miss York that cannot be delayed."

Lila frowned, and Knox wasn't dense enough not to understand that she wanted Miss York alone and now.

He turned to the woman of his every desire. "I will see myself out. Thank you for the knitting lessons. I hope we can do more of the same another time."

She nodded, her eyes bright and color still high. "I too, my lord. Thank you for calling on me."

Without further ado, he strode through the door and left the ladies to their own devices. The last words he heard before the front door closed behind him were from the Duchess of Derby on what on earth it was that she just interrupted.

EIGHT

Lila sat back on the settee where she had almost had her first kiss and watched as the Duchess of Derby shut the door and rounded on her. "Lila, what was that I just came upon? You were about to kiss Billington when you're supposed to be doing as your sister asked and be rid of him already."

Lila shushed her friend. "Keep your voice down before my aunt or her servants hear you," she chastised.

Hailey came and sat beside her, her eyes beseeching her for an answer. "Well, what is happening here? I almost caught you kissing the man."

A shiver ran down her spine at the thought of kissing him. Longing tore through her, knowing she had not done what she so wished. "I know what you almost witnessed. I lived it, and it was marvelous." She shook her head, slumping farther into the chair. "I'm a terrible person, am I not? I want him as much as he wants me, or at least who he thinks I am, and I cannot have him."

"Lila," Hailey said, compassion in her eyes. "He thinks you're someone else. You must tell him the truth," she pleaded.

"I fear it is too late for that. I agreed to let him try to persuade me into marrying him, and I worry that if I were myself and such a gentleman was courting me with such wicked temptations, I would have already succumbed to his charms. I have no governance when around him. What am I going to do?"

"You tried to tell him no when he asked you?"

"I did, yes, but as you know, he would not take that as my final answer, and now, with him being attentive, kind, and so very tempting, how am I to resist him? I want him for myself, and I cannot have him."

Hailey cringed, understanding dawning in her eyes. "This is a predicament. I can only suggest you try to keep your distance, but I know that will be difficult. These men, especially rakes, which Billington was once famous for being, have a way of tempting women such as ourselves in a manner that is nigh impossible to ignore."

"He almost kissed me, Hailey. His lips brushed mine, and something deep within me, a need, flickered to life in my belly. What was that, do you suppose?" she asked her married friend.

She would know more than her widow aunt what happened between a man and woman.

"Oh dear, this is most unfortunate. What you feel is desire, and that, my oldest friend, can lead you on a merry dance and a ruined reputation quicker than a quadrille."

Lila stared at her friend, taking in all that she said. "I know that I have to keep from falling under his charms, to stop myself from thinking all that he says to me is meant for me, not Harlow, but it is hard. I have always thought him handsome and kind. I have not admitted this to anyone, not even you, but I have always considered such a man to be the kind whom I would marry. Not that anyone has ever asked."

"Oh, Lila," Hailey said, pulling her into a tight embrace. "Do not despair. There is a man out in the world for you, just waiting for you to step into his path."

Lila nodded, swallowing the lump in her throat that told her otherwise. "What if my time has come and gone? What if this is my only chance of making a man I admire see me and fall in love so deeply that he does not care I'm not who he believes?"

Hailey sighed, her lips thinning into a dubious line. "He will be angry and feel betrayed. Played the fool when he finds out the truth. You must guard your heart, see the Season out, tell him no as planned, and leave."

Lila swiped at the lone tear that slid down her cheek. She wanted to rail at the world, scream at the unfairness of it all. She wanted to make him fall in love with her, not Harlow, but her. "I understand what you're saying, Hailey, and I love you for your frankness, but I'm not sure I can do that. If this is my final chance at happiness, I think I will step forward and try to catch the life I want." She could see the disappointment in her friend's eyes, and she hated that she did not agree with her on this plan. Not that she could blame her. She was being a little outlandish to continue what she was already doing with Billington. "He will either love me or despise me, but I can take that risk if it means I have some chance of winning his heart."

"The cost could be too great, Lila. I do not think you ought to do this," Hailey said. "But I understand that in life, we must make choices that are not always easy, and maybe Harlow was not for Billington, but you are. Maybe your wild plan will be seen as a gift to his lordship. Not right away, mind, but one day he may choose to forgive you this duplicity merely because he loves you so much."

Lila nodded. That was what she was counting on. God willing.

. . .

KNOX STOOD BESIDE HIS GOOD FRIEND Renford, watching with amusement as Miss York, the Duchess of Derby, and Viscountess Leigh stood together, deep in conversation. If he were a betting man, he would say the duchess and Miss York were trying to convince the viscountess of something. What that was, he could only imagine. Some profound ladies' business, he assumed.

"How is your courting of Miss York coming along? Since her return to town, she seems much changed. Less likely to give you the cut direct, which she often did before her departure, if my memory serves me correctly." Renford smirked, sipping his beer.

All true, unfortunately, and he was glad of the change of character. Miss York had been prickly at best before she returned from Grafton. He could only assume her parents and her sister had talked some sense into her and told her what a good catch he was and that she would be lucky to marry him. He would prefer that she came to that conclusion herself, but he would take any assistance offered to him at this point to win her hand.

Not that he wanted to boast about his worth or have others do so for him, but he was a kind man, rich, and ready to settle down. The Season's diamond would be the perfect jewel to add to his coffers.

"Does she not have a sister who is very similar in looks?" Renford asked him.

Knox nodded, remembering Miss Lila York. She had come to London the year after Derby had found his duchess, since they were best friends. Had he not been so disinterested in marriage, he may have felt inclined to court her. She was as stunning as her sister, if not more so, for she always had a kind word for anyone, no matter their station.

"She does, an older sister, but she has not come to town for several years now. I thought she had married, but I was mistaken."

Renford frowned at him. "You seem to know quite a lot about Miss York's older sister, who is not married and no longer visits London. Maybe you are courting the wrong sibling?"

Knox laughed at his friend's teasing, rolling his shoulders, not entirely comfortable with the knot in his gut that told him that maybe his friend had been right. Was he wrong courting the younger Miss York, considering up until recently she had shown no interest in him whatsoever? He ground his teeth. Too late to do anything about it now, he supposed...

"One must work with what is before him. It is unfortunate that the elder Miss York did not give herself another Season. I'm certain she would have found a husband by now."

"No doubt," Renford stated. "But you have

known the younger Miss York for some time, not just this Season."

"I know her very little at best. She attended a house party I held several years ago, the very one that resulted in Viscount Leigh finding his viscountess."

"Ah yes, the beautiful Woodville sisters. There is something in the water in Grafton. Here we have the York sisters, friends to the Woodvilles, and just as appealing. Although I cannot vouch for the elder Miss York, I shall have to believe your assessment of her magnificence." Renford smiled.

Knox shook the little bit of melancholy that plagued him. Whatever had happened when Miss York had traveled home? She was no longer so prickly toward him. Welcoming of his suit even. The thought gave him hope and told him more than any words could that he was doing the right thing. Courting the younger Miss York was what he wanted to do, and he would succeed in winning her hand.

NINE

T he following morning, those privileged enough to receive an invitation were asked to join Lord and Lady Merlov's family for a breakfast held at their home that backed onto the Thames.

Although not living in the most sought-after location of London for the *ton*, the family was extremely wealthy and their home one of the finest, and so each year, those lucky enough to score an invite made their way out of Mayfair to enjoy a morning held on grassy verges with large trees that shaded the immense, manicured yard.

Lila arrived with her friend, the Duchess of Derby, and her husband, thankful to be included in the opulent breakfast she had never attended when she was in London during her two Seasons.

They made their way through the house, stepping onto the terrace where the gardens came into their awe-inspiring view. They were as immaculate as the house, but with the added charm of sunshine reflecting off the sandstone home, making the terrace glow like gold.

"Lady Merlov has outdone herself this year. Look at all the flowers. The garden will smell like a hothouse of roses," Hailey said, smiling at Lila.

She took a deep breath, taking in the magnificent sight that so few got to experience. How lucky she was to have friends who attended such events and included her in them.

When she returned to Grafton, if she could not convince Lord Billington that he was meant for her and not her younger sister, she would miss all the excitement, the balls, parties, and friendships she would have to say goodbye to again.

Hailey's most especially.

They joined the host on the lawn and conversed for several minutes, but Lila's attention was not on what Lady Merlov was explaining. Rather her engagement was fixed elsewhere.

Lord Billington.

He stood beside the Duke of Renford, the two gentlemen smiling down at several young ladies who had cornered them by a large oak tree.

Renford looked pleased by the attention. Billington, on the other hand, appeared less so. Bored came to mind, and distracted, if his looking around was any indication. Was he searching for her?

He raised his brows at something Miss

Thorpe said before he spotted her over the young lady's coiffed locks. Lila raised her hand and waved without thinking, and pleasure flooded his features. Without waiting for a break in the conversation, he stepped away from the circle and started toward her.

Butterflies took flight in her stomach, and she breathed a deep, calming breath. Everything would work out in the end. He would be happy that she tricked him, for he would fall in love with her.

But what if he did not?

Oh dear, what if he hated her?

"Lord Billington," she said, dipping into a curtsy.

"Miss York," he replied. He picked up her hand and bestowed a lingering kiss on her gloved fingers. The need was back, and she fought to school her features and not give her emotions away.

When Harlow learned what she had planned instead of her intent, she would be terribly upset and furious at her. Unless her sister saw it as merely another means to be rid of his lordship. But how could she tell him the truth now? Certainly not before she knew if he loved her or not.

He thinks you're Harlow, Lila.

She inwardly cringed, her mind, wants, and needs all muddled together.

"You look as pretty as the flowers that are in

abundance here this morning. I'm glad you came. I was hoping you would."

"Were you?" she asked, taking her hand back from his, which he still held. "I thought you may be so very busy with your admirers that you would not know if I were here or not," she teased.

He turned and smiled at Renford, who continued to try to give each young miss the attention she required under the oak tree.

"Renford is a much better catch than I. He is already a duke. I'm only to become one someday," he said.

"From a distant family member, I understand. He never sired any sons, is that true?" They started along the terrace, slipping around the corner and into the much-welcome shade from the trellis above. Other guests mingled and sat at the circular tables placed there for their use.

"That is right. He was a distant cousin to my father, many times removed, and somehow remained a bachelor his whole life, and therefore by a stroke of luck, I shall inherit the title and everything that comes with it."

They sat at one of the tables, the scent of wisteria teasing Lila's senses. "Forgive me if I'm being more curious than I ought, but do you know the estate or what will be yours one day?"

He nodded, gesturing to a footman who placed a set of cups and saucers along with a teapot and a small plate of biscuits. "There is a

London town house on Grosvenor Square and a house in York. Much grander than mine and quite away from the Billington Estate. I have never been there, my relative is a solitary man now, and I do not want to disturb him, but it is a magnificent home. Sits before a large, man-made lake, a large water feature that runs merely by the use of gravity. Quite extraordinary, really."

Lila sighed. Easy to imagine such a beautiful home and location. York had so much history, namely the Romans, that was always interesting to explore and learn about. "And your home as the viscount. What is it like?"

He threw her a curious look, his head tipping to one side. "Miss York, do not tell me that you have forgotten my home so soon. You attended a house party there some years back. Do you not remember?"

Lila fumbled with the teapot, having forgotten that Harlow had attended a house party there with Isla Woodville, now Viscountess Leigh.

"Do forgive me. I have not forgotten," she said, wracking her brain to try to remember what Harlow had said about the house on her return home.

He chuckled, leaning back in his chair, studying her. "Well, I'm glad to hear it. I want to make an impression on you. Have you admire my estate and what I offer. I am, after all, trying to win your hand. It would be terrible form indeed should I not be able to impress you with my sizable assets."

Lila met his eyes, having the distinct feeling he did not only mean his houses and land by that statement. She nodded, feigning ignorance, and sipped her tea. "Well, I suppose you should know that I come with a dowry, as does my sister. A sizable one that I hope impresses you too, my lord." She grinned. "Since we're talking of what we would both bring to an understanding, even if that subject is taboo within the *ton*."

"Too true. We are being awfully vulgar, but then, where is the fun in life if one cannot be a little wild and push against the strains society places on us to test its limit?"

"I have the feeling you test your limits quite often. Or at least you used to before you turned your attention to me. I fear I have monopolized all your time."

"I like that you have monopolized me. I would like to monopolize you more."

Lila chuckled, relishing the morning even more. If only she could tell him who she was. Would he send her away, be angry or realize that with her, he could be happy?

"Really, my lord, do tell me how you could do that more than you already are. We spend most evenings together, and mornings too, it would seem. Any more time spent together and people will start to assume we're married already."

"Then I could spend the nights with you as well. What a lucky fellow I would be then, Miss York."

Heat kissed her chest and burned its way up her throat and onto her cheeks. Had he truly said such a scandalous thing? Not that it was not tempting to be with him so. To steal away at a ball or even a breakfast and let him kiss her.

Her first kiss and by a man whom she had always secretly coveted. And not just a brushing of lips this time, but a kiss to remember forever. That he thought her Harlow soured that thought somewhat, but she pushed it away. Harlow did not want him as a husband and had no romantic attachment to him in any way. But Lila did, and she was sure that he would have sought her out if she had been in town along with Harlow. She held on to that belief, not wanting to imagine otherwise.

"You should not say such things, my lord. You'll make me blush," she admitted.

"You're already blushing." He leaned close. "How beautiful you are when you do so too. You make my heart stop at the very sight of you."

Lila stared at him, having not known Billington had such wonderful, sweet words within him. Words that were spoken because of her interest and attention. She was the one who was here, and Harlow was not. It was Lila he talked to, declared himself before, no one else.

"Well," she mumbled, the heat on her cheeks scorching. "Now I'll look like I've had too much sun." She plopped a strawberry into her mouth, the sweet fruit as delicious as the man before her. "I will give you this, my lord. You are very good at being wicked and charming all rolled into one. Your years as a rake have paid off, I would say," she said, smiling.

His wicked grin made her blood run hot. "Rakes make the best husbands, or so I have been told. My wife will not be displeased. I can promise you that."

"Displeased how?" Lila asked, genuinely curious.

"Oh, my dearest Miss York, now that answer I cannot say, for there is a limit to my wickedness, and you have reached it."

Lila slipped another strawberry between her lips, watching him. His attention moved to her mouth, and she pouted, wanting to tempt him even more. "Well, that is a shame," she said. "Perhaps you're not a rake after all."

He growled, leaning back in his chair, his large hands stroking his legs. "Oh, I'm a rake, Miss York, and if you keep up your teasing, you will find out just how much of one I am."

If only she would.

TEN

K nox was walking a fine line between want and decorum, need and etiquette. He wanted the woman who sat before him, teased him unmercifully, and taunted him with her mouth.

Watching her pert lips cover the red fruit had almost been the tipping point of his restraint.

He liked the minx who had come back from Grafton, willing to allow him his courtship toward her. Her humor and her reactions to his sometimes-inappropriate words were sweet and merely made him want her all the more.

"May I ask you a question, Miss York?"

She nodded, slipping another dreaded strawberry into her mouth. "Of course," she said.

"May I call you by your given name? I have already given you leave to call me by mine." Her face paled, and he reached out, fear curdling his gut that perhaps she was ill. Or his request had insulted her in some way. "Are you well? You are very pale," he said. "I hope I have not offended you in any way. That was not my intent."

She shook her head, biting her lip. She glanced toward the lawns, and he saw her searching for her friends while thinking over his words. "I think I would prefer you call me Miss York," she said.

Knox tried to hide the disappointment her answer pulled forth, but he knew by her further distress he had failed miserably.

"I'm sorry." She reached out, touching his arm with her hand. "I have dispirited you by my answer." She bit her lip, frowning in thought. "I have never much liked my first name. What if I compromise, and you call me by an endearment," she suggested.

He raised his brows. "An endearment? Hmm." He thought on the idea a moment. "What about *Mon Amour*? Would that suit you well?" he asked, liking this idea better as it seemed even more intimate than her name.

"It would suit me very well." She smiled at him, and again he was struck by her beauty. He had never fallen for a woman before, not with his whole heart, but something told him Miss York, his *Mon Amour* was different. It was the start of something wonderful for him. For them both.

"Tell me of your home. Of course, I visited parts of Grafton for Derby's wedding, but I did not stay long. I understand your family owns a small estate there."

"My parents own a modest estate just outside of Grafton, but on the opposite side of town from the Woodvilles, whom you know already," she explained, a small, wistful smile on her lips. "I love Grafton, the people and close county we are, but that does not mean it doesn't come with the local meddling clergy or gossiping matron."

"I dislike gossip and lies. I do not see the point in spreading news that may or may not be true with no thought to those whom such words may injure." Knox amended his tone, not wanting to sound like an angry, judgemental rogue. He was not. He did not like it when people enjoyed other people's tribulations.

"Sometimes that's a little hard to avoid in small country towns like Grafton. But we live far enough out of the village not to be included too much in what is the latest on dit."

"I'm glad to hear it," he said.

She studied him a moment, her eyes narrowing in thought. "You sound like a man who's had a history with lies and has decided to be against gossip. Since we're getting to know one another a little more, would you be willing to tell me what happened to you in the past?"

Was he willing to tell her? His good school friend, the Duke of Romney, had been played a pretty fool by a handsome face and had almost lost his one true love from being repulsed by the same happening again. That was enough for him to never agree with liars or those who would pretend to get their way, even in a marriage.

"Nothing in my past has come to pass that has injured me directly. I merely speak of what I know and have seen in this fickle world of the *ton*."

"I'm happy you have not been injured before," she said. "Now that you know of my life in Grafton, what of yours where you grew up? Do you enjoy any particular sports?"

"I do, as a matter of fact. And as we're nearing the end of the Season, it gives me leave to ask you if you would like to have a day out with me and several of my friends. Have you ever been to Ascot for the races? We could make a day of it, enjoy a day in the sun with good company and horseracing."

"That sounds wonderful, my lord." Miss York turned to face him, the action placing her nearer to him than she had been before. She was but a small lean away from their lips touching, and he wanted to kiss her. To see if the feeling deep in his gut transferred to an intoxicating bond that only deepened when they kissed. The brush of their lips the day before had not been enough and had only teased him for what was to come.

The other guests sitting under the wisteria were not so close, but some were facing them, and he banked his desire for another time. A time when they were alone, and he may kiss her fully and for as long as she allowed him to.

"I have never been to Ascot, but I would love to attend with you." Her smile was sincere, and something in his chest beat hard. The woman before him had well and truly embedded herself under his skin, and he could only hope that he had done the same with her.

A LOUD BOOM OF THUNDER RATTLED THE windows, and Lila started in her chair before large, heavy drops of water began dripping through the vine-covered terrace. "Oh no, Lady Merlov's breakfast will be ruined."

Lord Billington stood, helping her to stand before they started to run for the nearest door. By the time they found one unlocked, people were laughing and screaming in equal measure as they tried to escape the unexpected summer downpour.

"So typical of English weather, is it not?" Lila dabbed at her face with the backs of her gloves, trying to dry herself as best she could, but she had a sinking feeling that she looked far from decent.

Lord Billington pulled out a handkerchief from his pocket and, without warning, dabbed her nose. "You had a little water droplet sitting there." He smiled, and Lila, for the first time, realized that the door they had escaped through was not one other guests had used.

She glanced about the space, a sitting room and one not in use for the party.

They were alone.

"Thank you," she managed, staring up at him. He was so handsome, even a little wet as he now was. He towered over her, and she couldn't help but admire the cut of his jaw or straight, aristocratic nose.

She wanted to kiss him. But kissing him would mean she took a further step down the forbidden road she had chosen to tread.

He studied her, his attention dipping to her lips. "I will admit that I have an overwhelming urge to kiss you, *Mon Amour*," he admitted.

She sucked in a startled breath, having not expected him to say such a wonderful thing, and no matter how bad or wrong it was, Lila wanted the same.

Her sister had placed her in this situation. It was Harlow's fault if blame were to be placed anywhere.

Not able to linger a moment longer, Lila closed the space between them and kissed him instead.

He pulled back but a moment, staring at her with no small amount of shock before he clasped her about the hips and wrenched her close. His lips took hers in a searing kiss that left her breathless. She grappled for purchase, clutched at the lapels of his coat, and kissed him back with as much expertise as she could find.

Which was not a lot, considering this was her first real kiss.

His tongue tangled with hers, sending her heart to pound. Lila pushed down the thought that he believed her to be someone else. Everything said between them since her arrival in town was her truth, no one else's, and she had to believe that should he have the choice, he would kiss her instead of Harlow.

His hands slipped over her back, making her skin prickle in awareness. She shivered, leaning into him farther, wanting to feel the heat from his chest, the heaving of his erratic breathing as their kiss delved deeper into the unknown, hotter, a wilder ride than anything she had ever experienced before.

He was addictive, and she always wanted to feel so loved. So full of pleasure that she could burst with excitement and joy.

He broke the kiss and stared down at her, pressing his forehead against hers. Their breaths mingled, and their hearts raced. She would never forget this day for the rest of her life.

A day that her life began, and hope beyond anything she had ever had in her six and twenty years awoke from slumber.

Her soul be damned. She could not deny herself a chance of happiness, of pleasure with Billington, even if that delight was born out of deceit.

ELEVEN

"Tell me when I can see you again," Knox demanded, wanting to spend more time and to be alone with Miss York and no one else.

"I'm attending the Collins ball this evening. Have you received an invitation?" she asked.

He nodded and guided her toward the door. The room led into the foyer, and a number of muffled voices could be heard discussing carriages and how long it would be before their vehicles would arrive to pick them up.

"I have, and if I can, may I request the first two dances with you? You in another man's arms is not how I would like our night to commence."

A blush kissed her cheeks, and he took the opportunity to steal another from her lips. She leaned into him, seeking his touch as much as he sought hers, and pleasure, hard and potent, tore through him.

She is a maid, not some wanton from the East End.

"You must return through this door, but I shall go outside and enter via the main terrace doors. It would not do your reputation any good to be seen alone in my presence."

"Very well," she agreed. "I will save you the first two dances, my lord."

"Knox, please. We're alone," he reminded her, wanting to hear his name on her lips.

"Knox then," she whispered, a small, wicked grin twisting up the sides of her mouth. "I look forward to seeing you this evening."

"Nothing will keep me away." He left her then, walking quickly to exit the room and leave no trace he was there with her. He came around the terrace, everyone who had been drenched from the passing shower inside and dripping water stains over the polished floors and Aubusson rugs.

"There you are," Renford said at his side. "If you think I missed where you raced Miss York to, you would be mistaken." His friend raised one teasing brow, and Billington chuckled. Could not hold back the grin on his lips, not even to save himself. "I stole my first kiss, my friend, and I have never wanted to kiss a woman again so much in my life. She is simply perfect." Her kindness, her humor, and seriousness, which he sometimes thought she believed too much in. But how lovely she was, and if he continued to receive kisses like the one just gifted, there was little chance she would turn down his offer of marriage. Again.

"She has not agreed to be your wife yet. Do not be so bold with her that you compromise the chit, and then you're forced to become her husband. She will resent you for the rest of your days."

"Point taken," he agreed, not wanting that situation to pass. "But my good man," he said, clapping Renford on the back. "I believe I was her first kiss, and let me tell you, her ability and quick tutelage makes me long for our wedding night. I think it will be wondrous."

"Oh dear lord, she has already said no once. You are very confident she will change her mind."

A woman who kisses a man such as Miss York kissed him did not deny herself long the enjoyment of the marriage bed. She would marry him and be all the happier for it. He could understand she wanted to be sure, and he was willing to give her time, but that did not mean he would not attempt to seduce her to his way.

"She will not say no. Her kiss told me so." Knox caught sight of Miss York with the Duchess of Derby and Viscountess Leigh who had also joined them, all three moving toward the Merlov's estate's doors. It seemed the breakfast was over for another year.

"Are you attending the Collins ball this evening? I should imagine you'll be continuing your seductive plans there as well," Renford drawled as they too made their way toward the doors, where carriage after carriage picked up its charges before moving on.

Excitement thrummed in his veins at the thought of seeing Miss York again. His *Mon Amour* as she was to be called. Why she did not want to use Harlow eluded him. The name suited her very well, but she had not given him leave to use her given name, and he would take what he could if it pleased her.

"I am going to be in attendance. Lord Collins always has a card room set aside for the gentlemen if you would like a game of Vingt-un before the ball is in full swing."

"Will that not displease your lady?" Renford teased.

"I have secured the first two dances. Any more than that, and we shall become the talk of the *ton*, and I wish to avoid that at all costs, thank you very much. You know how much I hate gossip and untruths, and they'll hound Miss York so much about our courtship that it may turn her off the union altogether."

"Very true," Renford agreed. "Or merely remind her that she has already said no and should do so again."

Knox threw his friend a displeased glare and

ignored his words. She would not be swayed against him, not after what happened earlier. The blood in his veins still pumped hard and strong at the memory of her kiss.

He would try to steal another.

Tonight.

LILA HAD NO SOONER STEPPED UP INTO the carriage with Hailey and Isla before they pinned her to her seat with displeased glares of equal measure.

"Where were you?" Hailey demanded to know. "You ran indoors, but not where everyone else ran to, and I could not find you. Not until several minutes later and when Lord Billington too reappeared."

"As if by magic," Isla drawled, her lips thinned into a judgemental pout.

"Where is the duke?" Lila asked instead, not wanting to answer their questions just yet.

"Heading to his club," Hailey said. "Now never mind my husband, answer my question, Lila," she demanded.

"I have decided, ladies, and you may hate me and not wish to be friends with me after this... Heavens, my sister may never speak to me again. Or she could, depending on how she views my actions here in London. Only time will tell. But this may be my last chance at happiness, and I intend to try to reach for it and see how the cards play out."

"You cannot do such a thing." Isla gasped. "Lord Billington will be crushed, feel like you played him the fool if you continue down this duplicitous road. You must stop."

"Lila, do think on this," Hailey beseeched. "We do not want you to be hurt in this situation either. I know Harlow had good intentions sending you here, but she did not consider the feelings you kept hidden away for Lord Billington for many years. She would never have asked you such a thing should she have known how you really felt." Hailey reached out, taking her hand. "If you cannot tell him to his face, you must send a letter to his lordship, explain all your wrongdoings and return home and then mayhap come back next year for the Season, try to tempt Lord Billington then. But this time as yourself, not your sister."

Hailey's suggestion was not an entirely bad one. She could tell Lord Billington everything she had fooled him with and why thus far and return to London next year, playing herself this time to try to get his lordship to see her instead of pining for her sister.

But she had kissed him, and he thought her to be Harlow...

Lila swallowed the lump in her throat as all she had done, the lies and pretending, crashed down on her like a boulder. "He's going to hate me when he finds out, you are right. I cannot tell him now." Panic assailed her, and she pulled off her gloves and fanned her face with her hands. "What have I done? I should never have listened to Harlow. I have few options, I can either tell him the truth and risk his reaction, or I play out this foolery and break his heart at the end of the Season like some teasing wanton East End whore."

Hailey sat straight, pinning her to her seat with her steely gaze. "What do you mean by that, Lila? What have you done?"

"What do you mean?" Isla gasped yet again, covering her mouth with her hand. "What is afoot that I do not know?"

Shame replaced the panic, and Lila cringed. "I kissed his lordship this afternoon." A kiss she had hoped to repeat, but how could she now? She needed to be truthful, but being so was far harder than she ever thought it would be. "And he kissed me back, but now I feel ill over it all. I'm doomed. My reputation, my sisters, everything will be lost over this foolish plan."

"I know you wanted a love match, my friend, and I want that for you too. We both do," Hailey said, gesturing to Isla. "But this is not the way to gain one. Please tell his lordship. You will see that all will be well in the end, and he will forgive you."

"And if he does not, then he never deserved to have you and see how wonderful you are in the first place," Isla mentioned, coming to sit beside her and taking her hand. "We will stand beside you and not let you fall, Lila. But you must be honest."

Lila sighed, the monumental task ahead of her almost too much. So much so that she wanted nothing more than to run home, pack, and flee like the coward she was.

"Very well. I shall tell his lordship. I will ensure we speak tonight, and I will explain everything to him. He will hate me for it, but you are right. This is for the best."

"It is dearest. Trust in what you feel for him and believe what he feels for you, and in time all will work out well."

Lila nodded. "I hope you're right." But the churning of her stomach told her Hailey was not. Not this time.

TWELVE

Knox spied Miss York in the crushing crowd of the Collins ball before she located him. This evening she wore a green silk taffeta gown that brought out the vibrant color of her eyes. The dress hugged her womanly form and accentuated all the parts that he loved on a woman most. Her bosom in particular...

The urge to steal her away someplace in this large home almost overrode his enjoyment of simply watching her with Lady Leigh, Miss York's closest friend.

Or so he had thought, but she had been spending a great deal of her time with the Duchess of Derby, so perhaps he had been wrong.

The dancing had not yet commenced, and he made his way to the card room, only to see Renford not yet in attendance. Forgoing his game of cards, he started toward his sole purpose for being here.

Her eyes sparkled with delight when he came into view, and he bowed, unable to mask the pleasure she brought forth in him.

"Good evening, Miss York. May I say how utterly beautiful you look this evening?" He took her hand, wishing her silk glove was not denying him the feel of her soft skin against his lips.

"Thank you, Lord Billington. You, too, look quite the gentleman this evening. And I see, somehow in the Season's chaos, you have managed to wear a green waistcoat to suit my gown. How providential."

"Providential indeed." He laughed as the first notes of a minuet sounded. "Shall we?"

She placed her hand in his, and he led her onto the floor, along with many other keen dancers. He pulled her into his arms as soon as the music allowed and relished having her back where she belonged.

Had it only been this morning that he had kissed the woman before him? It seemed like an age, and tonight he would do so again.

"Was your day as pleasant as mine? I must admit that after this morning, I did little but count down the hours until we would meet again." He hoped he was not too forward, but his words were the truth. He very much liked Miss York, more so than anyone he had ever met, and he wanted her to know such truths. How would she make up her mind to marry him or not if she did not know or trust his words?

"I had a pleasant day, my lord," she returned, a small tremor to her words that he could discern.

He turned her in the dance before they moved back within other couples for several steps. "Is something the matter, Miss York? You seem a little distracted." He paused. "I hope what happened between us earlier today has not upset you. That was not my intention."

"No," she shook her head, and tears pooled in her eyes. "It was not the kiss," she whispered.

Dread knotted in his gut, and he maneuvered them out of the multitude of dancers and eventually off the dance floor. "Meet me in the library, and we will talk. I do not want to see you so upset."

She nodded and parted from him, slowly making her way through the guests. Knox did the same, but in the opposite direction. He slipped through a door in the ballroom that led to a darkened passage used by servants, he guessed, before making his way to the library, where hopefully he could repair whatever was troubling her and put her concerns aside.

LILA FOUND THE LIBRARY AND MOVED TO the low-burning fire to wait for Lord Billington.

Nerves bombarded her stomach, and she took a deep breath, worried she would cast up her accounts.

A sliver of light entered the room as his lordship joined her before it was snuffed out as the door closed. He strode toward her, handsome as ever, and a pang of regret pierced her heart.

How she wished he strode purposefully toward her knowing she was Lila and not Harlow. But he did not. He thought her someone else, and it was time she stopped playing with his heart so cruelly.

How she could have thought pretending to be someone else was a good sentiment, she would never comprehend.

He clasped her shoulders, staring at her as if to pull the truth from her lying lips.

"What has happened? Have I offended you, and there is no way to right my wrong?" he asked, a small frown between his dark brows.

"No, you have not offended me. I shall always cherish the kiss we shared, but there is something you should know."

"What is it, *Mon Amour*?" he asked, his attention dipping to her lips before meeting her eyes.

If this were the last chance she would have to be with him, to touch and kiss him, she would be heedless one last time before telling him the truth. A reality that would send him from her, hating her, from this day forward.

"I would like you to kiss me again," she said, damning herself forever.

A wicked grin lifted the sides of his lips, and he did not hesitate to do as she asked. He wrenched her into his arms, tipping up her chin with his hand, and lowered his lips to hers with a torturous, unhurried pace.

The moment they touched, fire coursed through her blood, removing all guilt over what she was doing, what she had asked from him.

His mouth took hers in a searing kiss, and she held on to him to keep herself from swooning at his feet.

He was overbearing, fire in her arms, demanding and yet, also not so as well. An enigma she could not entirely understand.

"You taste like sin," she whispered.

His hand slipped lower on her back, clasping her bottom, and she bit her lip, having never been pressed against a man in such a scandalous manner before. The emotions, the feelings that tingled and ached in places that she had never known existed made her want him to touch her more. Pet and stroke her in all those aching places.

What was wrong with her to think like this? What had happened to the clear-thinking, over-the-hill old maid from Grafton?

She did not recognize herself, nor did she like herself very much right now.

The door to the room opened, and Lila tumbled back as Lord Billington dropped her. Still, it wasn't quick enough, for Lord Collins and several other gentlemen entered the library, cheroots in mouth and smiling at their ability to disappear from the ball undetected.

Not unlike Lila and Lord Billington's ability. The shocked countenance of Lord Collins and the bright-eyed, humorous expressions of the others, who knew they had walked in on something utterly unacceptable, made the pit of her stomach wrench.

"Lord Billington, is that you?" Lord Collins asked, and before he could reply, several other gentlemen strode from the room back toward the ballroom, their quickened footsteps a drum against her ears and their mission clear for all present.

No doubt, within a matter of minutes, the news of her scandalous liaison with Lord Billington in the library would be the *ton's* latest on dit and the fodder for gossip for weeks to come.

"It is, Lord Collins. I'm here with Miss York, who's agreed to become my bride. Will you not congratulate us?" he asked them.

The room spun, and Lila clutched at Lord Billington's arm to stop herself from swooning. What was he saying?

Marriage?

To her?

He does not know who I am.

"Is this true, Miss York?"

Lila could feel Lord Billington's hardened stare against her cheek, and she knew why. If she did not marry him, did not say that she was indeed just proposed to, her reputation and that of Harlow's would be ruined forever.

The muscles in his arms tensed the longer she remained unable to form words, and she stared at Lord Collins, her tongue feeling as though it was swollen and heavy with more mistruths she was about to utter.

"Harlow?" Lord Billington urged.

She met his eye, and the concern she read there told her he was thinking the same as she. That they had been caught, and there was little else for him to do other than be the gentleman he was raised to be and offer her his hand in marriage.

She nodded and swallowed hard. "It is true, Lord Collins. Please congratulate us and congratulations on being the first to know our wonderful news," she said, relieved that her words came out joyful, instead of sullen and shamed.

Lord Collins clapped his hands, striding toward them with a large smile on his elderly visage. "Felicitations my friends," he said, just as several other people milled into the room as if to still catch Lord Billington and herself in an improper situation.

Lila allowed Lord Collins to buss her cheeks before she stood aside and watched him energetically shake Billington's hand. "Well, this is a coup for me and Lady Collins. Lord Billington is a fine catch, Miss York, and for a young lady such as yourself to earn his respect and love, well, we're very happy for you. And pleased the announcement will occur under our roof." His lordship paused, turning back to those near the door, watching everything come to pass. "Now, let us return to the ball. There is much to celebrate."

Lord Billington took her hand, laying it on his arm as they followed Lord Collins and others who had hoped to take part in their downfall. Not that there would be no gossip from what had occurred here this evening, but Lord Collins's excitement and belief over what had happened in his library would go a long way in tamping down too much scandal.

On the other hand, her scandal and lie were not something she wanted to face, and now it would seem she had no choice but to tell him the truth and see if he still wished to marry her after that fact.

Or let her succumb to the downfall she brought upon herself.

THIRTEEN

S he was living a lie, and yet still, she could not stop herself from enjoying the little time she had with Billington within this cocoon of bliss while it lasted. The following evening at the Davies ball, Knox swept Lila out of the ballroom. Lila fought back laughter as they raced through the garden and around the large estate until they came to the front steps.

"Wait here. I'll fetch my carriage, and we shall leave."

Lila wrenched him back, stopping him from fleeing. "But I cannot. Hailey will wonder where I am and will worry."

"She saw us together. She will know you're with me."

Lila threw him a skeptical look. Even if Hailey did think she was with Billington, that made her as far from safe as anyone. She had assured her friends she would tell him the truth

TAMARA GILL

when the time was right, no matter the consequences. But she so wanted to be with him.
Alone and without the prying eyes of London
watching their every move.

Not that she should want such a thing. She
had accepted his proposal under false as-
sumptions.

What a disaster she had become.

He stole a quick kiss that left longing raging
through her before he left her to order his carriage from a waiting footman. Billington lingered
patiently for the carriage to come around,
speaking to guests who came and went from the
ball as if nothing was awry.

Lila huddled in the shrubbery, not wanting
to be seen. To be caught lurking in the dark and
waiting to flee with a viscount who was not yet
her husband would be a disaster. But the thought
of being alone with him was far from a cata-
strophe and overrode all her good sense.

A carriage rolled to a stop before the viscount, and he leaned up to the driver, whispering
something in the older man's ear before the driver
nodded in understanding.

Billington climbed up into the carriage, and
it rolled to a stop before her. Without a word, the
door opened, and checking one last time no one
was in view from the town house door, Lila
bolted from the gardens and climbed up into the
equipage.

She laughed at their antics. They were absurd, and this was all immoral, but she could not stop herself from clasping the little bit of happiness this time with Billington afforded her.

He moved across the carriage and came to sit beside her. Without a word, he wrapped her in his arms, tipping her head back to stare at her with such affection that her heart raced.

She clasped the lapels of his coat, grounding herself in any way that she could.

"Now I have you all to myself." His deep baritone washed over her, warm and comforting, and she huddled closer to him.

"And I you," she admitted, tightening her hold on him.

"I want to kiss you," he admitted, his lips but a breath from hers.

Lila could smell the brandy on his breath and the scent of sandalwood, the two odors forever embedded in her mind to be Billington. She knew no matter where she went in life or what happened after her time here in London that whenever she smelled those scents, she would think of him and their time together.

Stolen as it was.

"I want you to kiss me too." Lila did not wait for him but pushed forward, taking his lips instead. His mouth seized hers in a kiss that left her grappling for breath.

She moaned when their tongues tangled,

making the pit of her stomach clench in the most delectable way. Warmth and wonder bombarded her mind, and she lost herself in his arms. Never wanting to be found if this was the pleasure he wrought on her soul.

Somewhere during the kiss, it changed, morphed into something wicked and wild. Lila undulated against him, unable to halt what her body craved.

He heard her silent plea and did not disappoint. His touch wandered from her hip, slicing across her stomach to push against her there. But it wasn't enough. She craved his touch, desiring him with reasoning and need she did not understand.

"What are you doing to me?" she gasped.

He broke the kiss, gifting her a sinful grin before his hand slid farther along her body to cup her mons through her gown. She gasped, the ache he ignited like a fire she could not extinguish.

"Let me touch you, *Mon Amour.*"

Lila could not deny him, not anything. She nodded, and his lips took hers. She lost herself in his kiss, in his touch. The breath of cool air bussed her ankles and knees before his hand, hot and determined, ran along her thigh, squeezing it and making her ache even more with hunger.

He pushed her legs apart, and she gasped, breaking the kiss when his hand slipped along her mons. Liquid heat spilled from her, and he moaned and swore under his breath before rubbing her with his fingers. Lila closed her eyes and lost herself in the exquisite sensation. His touch was soft but skilled, and before she could think twice, she opened her legs farther, allowing him access to her most private parts.

"Do you like this?" he asked, kissing along her neck to the underside of her chin.

"Mmhmm, very much," she answered. She bit her lip, not quite understanding what her body wanted or needed but knowing this wasn't enough. She wanted more.

"Do you want me to stop? There is so much I can show you, but only if you want me to."

Lila reached down and lay her hand over his, pushing his touch against her, igniting a promiscuous sensation through her that would not be sated.

"I want more. I want everything," she admitted, having never meant her words more in her life.

"Then I shall give you what you want," Knox said, fighting to control the desire that rioted through him like a wildfire.

He wanted to please her, to give her everything she wanted. She watched him stroke her wet cunny and tease her. He wanted to taste her with his tongue, and he would. One day, but not this night. Tonight this would be enough and the start of more to come.

He caressed her, teased her dripping heat with his finger, before pushing just the tip of his digit inside. He felt her tense about his hand, and he bit back a curse. Damn it all to hell. He wished it was his cock where his hand was right at this moment.

He was rigid and weeping himself, and should she touch him, he could lose all self-control.

And then the softest of caresses pressed against his cock. Knox swore, ripping her hand away. "No, *Mon Amour*. Tonight is just for you," he said, hoping she would hear the ache in his voice and how close he was to losing the little scrap of control he wielded upon himself.

She shook her head, determined as ever. "No, I want you to feel how I do, too," she argued.

"I can take care of myself in the comfort of my bed. Later, not now. This night is just for you," he stated, hoping she would not try again.

But she did, and he could not force her hand away, no matter how much he knew he should. She stroked him through his breeches, and he fought not to spend like a young man new to sexual pleasures. Her touch was so good. What he had craved since the first moment she kissed him.

"I want to make you feel how you're making me feel," she said.

Knox did not know when he lost control of the situation, but before he could deny her request, she had straddled his lap, and her wet, exposed cunny was rubbing up against his breeches.

All thought of denying her anything fled from his mind. He clasped her ass, squeezed her soft mounds, and wrenched her against him. But it wasn't enough. He wanted everything he could not have.

He set her back a little on his legs and ripped his falls open. His cock sprang into his hand, and he stroked it before her, watching as her eyes widened with wonder and awe.

"Oh my," she said, licking her lips and making him groan. She would be the end of him for certain.

"I'm not going to ruin you, *Mon Amour*. But I want you to come against me. Not against my breeches, which may be too rough for your precious cunny. My cock will be smoother for you."

She nodded, her tongue licking her lips as she wiggled against him. Her eyes widened in wonder as she pressed against him. Warm and soft fused with velvet steel. There was nothing better in the world.

"Damn it, that feels too good," he croaked. She took charge, wrapping her arms about his neck and moving against him like a well-seasoned whore.

But this was no whore he held wrapped in his arms. This was the woman he was going to marry. The woman who had stolen more of him than any woman ever had before in his life.

She kissed him, and he allowed her to do what she willed. She rocked against him, her hot, needy cunny pushing his cock, seeking the release they both aspired to.

He held her, helped her ride him without taking her innocence, and never had he ever had such a fulfilling, igniting sexual experience in his life.

He was on the precipice of spending against her, of lifting her just the slightest bit to impale her on his manhood. Just the thought almost pushed him over the edge.

She cast back her head. Her bottom lip lodged firmly between her teeth as she rode him in the untutored dance of lovemaking. "Oh, Billington," she moaned. "Oh my, I've never—"

He kissed her, hard and long, stroked her tongue with his, and swallowed her screams as her orgasm rocked through her. Her muffled moans were a Siren's song that wrapped around him like a net.

"*Mon Amour*," he gasped, his balls tightening, his cock extending before he came hard and long against her sweet mons.

They sat like that for several minutes before their breaths came back into sync. "That was beyond anything I have ever known," she breathed, clasping his cheeks and tipping up his face to meet her eyes.

He stared at her, unable to comprehend the beautiful woman in his arms. "You are remarkable," and you are mine, knowing right at that moment that he could never watch her marry another.

FOURTEEN

L ila stood at the window in the front foyer of her aunt's home the following morning, her mind a whirl of memories, of feelings of what had occurred the night before.

She was engaged to a man who did not know who she was.

"I'm so very happy for you, my dear," her aunt said for the hundredth time after being told the news the night before. "Oh, your mama will be so happy. I shall write to them today."

Lila smiled at her aunt. When her mother discovered what she and Harlow had done, there would be hell to pay.

Even so, knowing how wrong her actions had been, Knox's touch had lit a flame within her soul that she did not want to douse. If anything, she wanted to stoke that fire and make it burn brighter than ever.

"Oh my darling, could this day be any hotter?" her aunt complained on her way to the rear parlor of the home, still shadowed in the morning sun. Come the afternoon, however, that room too would be warm and uncomfortable.

"The weather is parching indeed," she replied, knowing she had been burning hot the night before and loving every moment of it.

A curricle rolled to a stop before the town house, and excitement thrummed through her veins when she recognized Billington. He jumped down with ease before handing the reins to his footman, who sat on the rear seat.

Lila quickly moved to the stairs, not wanting him to think she had been waiting for him, for she had not. She had not known he would call on her today, but now that he had, all thoughts of the uncomfortable weather fled from her mind.

A quick knock on the door and the butler answered, throwing her a curious look when she merely kept standing on the staircase without purpose.

Lord Billington stepped into the foyer, his wide smile when he spied her making the butterflies in her stomach come to life.

"Miss York, how very good to see you again. I thought I might steal you away this morning for a pleasure ride in my curricle. But only if your aunt can spare you."

Time alone with his lordship was what she wanted most, and before she could ask her aunt, she heard her quickened steps along the parquetry floor.

"Good morning, Lord Billington. May I offer congratulations again, my lord, on your betrothal to my niece? I'm sure she would enjoy a pleasant drive out with you today. How kind you are to offer."

"Not kindness at all, Mrs. Chapman. As Miss York is now my intended, I would like nothing more than her company, and I have a new curricle I would like to take out and enjoy. But only if you approve it, of course," he said, his voice as sweet as wine.

Her aunt tittered at his lordship's charm. "I see no harm in an outing, but take a bonnet, my dear. You do not want to burn before the opera this evening."

"Of course, Aunt," Lila said, turning back to Billington. "I will fetch my hat and gloves and meet you directly at the carriage.

Before waiting for a reply, she ran to her room, found everything she required for her outing with his lordship, and soon took his hand and stepped up into the high equipage, ready for their adventure.

She nestled against him, wrapping her arm in his, which he took no issue with. "I'm so happy you called, my lord. Do tell me where you're taking me today."

"Well, as to that, you will have to keep a secret, for if we're caught, it will ensure a scandal unlike any London has ever known."

"Really?" she asked, even more intrigued. She smiled up at him, and the urge to lean close and steal a kiss almost overwhelmed her propriety.

"Yes, really." He wiggled his brows, and she chuckled, enjoying her time alone with him already. They headed out of London and were soon traveling on the road to Bath.

"Where are we going?" she asked. A little trepidation ran through her that he would not return her to town before their absence was noted.

"I have a small cottage on the outskirts of London. It's where I go when the Season becomes too much. No one knows of it other than you," he said, meeting her eyes.

She inwardly sighed, appreciating that he trusted her above anyone with his secret. "I will not tell anyone of your refuge," she said.

"I would not doubt it a moment." The carriage rattled along the road, with both lost in their thoughts for a moment. "On my small estate, a river runs through it and into the Thames. I've made many adjustments to my boathouse that overlooks the river, and now it's a safe and secure place to swim if one wants. I thought you may want to participate in such a pastime today. And enjoy the picnic that I promised you. It is awfully warm, after all, and we're sure to get ravenous."

"Swimming? Really!" She had not taken part in the sport for years, and thinking of taking a refreshing dip into cool, calm water was heavenly indeed. "I would love that above anything. But I have nothing to change into later."

"There is a small boathouse that I had built that holds most things people wish to use when swimming. We may go punting too if you wish."

"I would prefer to swim," she said, the day growing even more thrilling than she first thought. "Will you swim with me if I do?" she asked, not wanting to go alone.

He chuckled. "Nothing would stop me from joining you. Not even if I could not swim."

AFTER CHECKING IN AT HIS COTTAGE AND notifying his staff—who lived permanently at the estate—that he was heading down to the riverside for the afternoon, they carried on with their journey. But not before he ordered refreshments and a light lunch to be delivered and served in the boathouse. Which, in all truth, wasn't a boathouse at all.

It resembled an extension of the Georgian manor house but with an oversized terrace that overlooked the running river before them.

Miss York's gasp told him she thought it as

TAMARA GILL

charming as he did and pride washed through
him that she favored it. He wanted her to like
everything about him, including his estates and
what he could offer her.

Not only his hand, but status, wealth, and
homes as pretty as this one to raise their children, to live and laugh, and enjoy life to the
fullest.

He pulled the carriage up under a shady tree
and helped her alight. They started over to the
boathouse and he could see that it was just as he
left it last. The terrace was clean of leaves and de-
bris, the windows sparkling in the mid-morning
sun.

"It is lovely," she said, slipping her hand
into his.

Knox had never had a woman reach for him
in such an innocent way, and he liked that she
trusted him enough to do so. To be with him and
not deny him some time away from the *ton*, to be
with her alone.

"I know it's scandalous of me to bring you
here without a chaperone. Your aunt would have
my head if she knew I had stolen you away to my
private estate."

She chuckled, stepping up on the stone terrace to stroll to the front of the boathouse that
overlooked the river. From here, one could dive
into the cool running water or sit on the terrace
and soak one's feet. Or, if preferred, there were

reclining chairs with big, soft cushions to lay upon and sleep the lazy days away.

"I think I could spend the rest of my days here and be quite content," she said. "I have not swum in years. It's not ladylike if you did not know."

"Do you think you'll remember how to?" he asked, pulling at his cravat before undoing his waistcoat.

"I do. We learned to swim at the Woodville Estate and I'm sure I have not forgotten. We all grew up together, you see, and they have a river on their estate and a swimming area that the family often used."

"You had a happy childhood then?" he asked, laying his coat and waistcoat over a chair. He wrenched his shirt over his head. He knew he should not undress before her, but then, he had been a lot more intimate with her already and wanted her to see him.

See what could be hers when she married him. He was not shy about tempting her to his bed before their vows were said.

"The most wonderful childhood with lots of laughter and friends. It is what I wanted for myself when I married, but I suppose that ship has sailed," she said.

He frowned, coming up to her. "Your ship merely needed to sail into my port. Which it did in Lord Collins's library."

Her eyes widened before she flung back her head and laughed. It was an expression of surprise and joy all rolled into one, and he wanted to hear her laugh just so more often.

"You have no shame, do you, my lord?"

"Knox, *Mon Amour.*"

"Knox, then," she repeated, turning to give him her back. She glanced over her shoulder, meeting his gaze quickly, and he could see the challenge in her eyes. "Help me with my buttons...Knox," she said suggestively.

He slipped his hands atop her hips, pulling her against his chest. Her bottom hit his cock, and already he felt himself growing hard. "With pleasure." He took the opportunity to kiss her neck and felt the shiver run down her spine before concentrating on the task at hand.

He could undress a woman with skill, and it did not take him long to undo her many buttons.

The gown slipped from her shoulders, along with her corset, both pooling at her feet.

She turned and faced him, kicking off her slippers and stockings. "Are you ready?" she asked him, a teasing smile on her lips.

He nodded. "After you, Miss York." Taking the opportunity to admire the view as she dived into the water, he followed close on her heels not a moment later.

FIFTEEN

Lila swam and laughed at the sound of Billington jumping in after her. She squealed in delight as his hands wrapped about her waist, pulling her against him.

"I have caught you," he declared, spinning her about.

She wrapped her arms around his neck, unable to remove the smile from her lips. "So it seems," she said, running her hands through his wet hair and pushing it from his face.

She liked to look at him, admire his handsomeness. She wanted him to be hers. Why could he not have courted her instead of her sister? Everything would be so different. Or at least so much easier.

Lila pushed from him, flicking up some water to splash Billington. "Do you think you can catch me again?" she taunted, trying to swim away. He caught her foot and dragged her back toward him.

"I will never let you get away, *Mon Amour.*"

Warmth spread through her, even though the water was cooler than she thought it would be, considering the hot day. He was so charming and lovely and everything she had always dreamed of in a husband.

And now she was to marry him under false pretenses.

She shuddered at the thought of telling him the truth. He would be angry and hurt. After all that they had done together, the many kisses and touches. He would not understand the lie, and rightfully so.

Harlow had stated she had done nothing with Lord Billington, that the chemistry was not there, so surely he knew, somewhere deep down, that she was different than before.

His perfect match.

Lila wrapped herself around him. The feel of their wet bodies, his strong, muscular lines pressed against her with very little keeping them apart.

Her shift was all but transparent. She ran her hands over his chest, enjoying the sense of him under her palms. "You feel so good, Knox," she said, using his given name.

His gaze burned, and she shivered, the need to be with him again, to experience how he had made her feel the night before, overriding all self-control.

Lila pulled herself closer to him and kissed him. He took but a moment before he kissed her back with such passion, with such an intoxicating appetite, she struggled to remain rational.

"You feel like heaven in my arms." One of his hands clasped her bottom and squeezed it, pulling her against his growing manhood.

"Mmmm," she moaned, rolling her hips against him. "Whatever do you do to me? You've made a wanton out of me, and I'm not myself."

His chuckle resembled more of a growl. "I cannot get enough of you either. You're all I think about night and day. You occupy my dreams, taunting me with your nearness that when I awake, and you're not there, my heart hurts at your absence."

Lila had never heard such sweet words. Being with him was intoxicating and made her forget why she was sent to London. How could she break his heart when she wanted to occupy it, hold it forever against hers, and keep it safe?

"Knox," she sighed, wishing she could tell him more. Tell him everything, but she could not. She could not risk that he would hate her. "You make it so hard to deny you anything."

He spun her about in the water, and she laughed. "You gave me until the end of the Season to make you fall in love with me. To say yes to me. Now that the choice has been taken from you, that does not mean I still do not want to win your heart. Do I hear that your walls are starting to crack and crumble to my constant battering?" he asked, his eyes merry with laughter.

"Perhaps they are. A very little."

"Humph," he said. "I think you're being modest with that statement. I think I'm going to win this little competition of ours."

She wished he could win. She hoped he knew which heart he had already stolen. "Nothing is assured, Knox. You ought not to be so confident."

He dipped them into the water, staring at her, his eyes taking in her every feature. "I want you to know that I've never felt the way I do when I'm with you. You have made me feel things I never thought were for me in this life." He paused, staring at something over her shoulder but a moment before catching her eyes. "I think... no, I know," he amended. "That I've fallen in love with you, *Mon Amour.*"

Lila lost the capacity to breathe, and she reached up, clasping his strong jaw. He was looking at her as if she held all the power to his happiness in the palm of her hand. And she wasn't sure she did not. Unfortunately, along with that hope was also despair over her actions toward him.

"I've fallen in love with you too, Knox," she

said, cursing herself to Hades. Overwhelming happiness mixed with horror at what she had declared. He did not know who exactly he loved, and she was a monster to let him believe what he did. To express herself when she had no right to say anything at all.

He took her lips in a searing kiss, and she shoved aside the little voice in her head that told her this was wrong. She knew that, and she would pay for what she had done. But not this day. Not right now. Not when he was kissing her as if she were the beginning and the end of everything good in the world.

HE LOVED HER, AND HE HAD DECLARED himself. For the first time in his life, he had told a woman he loved her, not merely because he required her to marry him but because he meant every word.

His body thrummed with renewed power at the thought of what their future would be like. How wonderful their life would be. Love matches in the *ton* were few and far between, and after first meeting Miss York, he had not thought she wanted one moment of his time.

But something had changed along the way, and now... Well, she wanted every part of him, including his heart.

Their tongues tangled, and he walked them

back toward the paved terrace, wanting to give her all he could without taking too many liberties before their marriage. But he had to taste her, be with her as much as he could.

They came to the dock, and he broke the kiss. "Would you like a light repast? My servants have delivered our lunch, I can see."

He glanced into the boathouse and spied the small table with a bouquet of small wildflowers sitting at its center.

"I am quite parched," she said, swimming over to the steps and climbing up onto the terrace.

Knox followed her, enjoying the sight of her bottom that was visible through the sheer, wet material of her shift. He grinned, wondering if she knew her gown was transparent. Something about the way she walked into the boathouse, her hips swaying seductively, told him she did.

He moved past her and pulled out her chair. She smiled, picked up a glass of wine, and drank it before setting it back on the table.

"I said I was parched," she all but hummed, her voice a seductive tenor he'd not heard before. A tone that made his cock stand on end and his heart thump hard in his chest. "But I'm hungry for something else entirely, other than food."

Knox growled, wrenching her into his arms and taking her sweet lips in a kiss that left them both breathless. He bent down, hoisted her onto his shoulder, and carried her to the large daybed that sat before an unlit hearth.

He tossed her onto the cushioned bed, and she laughed as she bounced. So beautiful, so carefree and his.

His heart.

He crawled up the bed, pushing her to lie on her back. "Do you want to feel wonderful again, my love?"

She watched him under hooded eyes but nodded. "What do you have in mind?" she asked, biting her bottom lip.

His cock strained for release. Without uttering a word, he kneeled at her feet and set her legs apart. A light blush kissed her cheeks, but she did not try to stop him.

He slid her wet shift up her long legs, kissing her cool, soft skin behind her knee, between her thighs, and her stomach as the material pooled about her waist.

Her breathing hitched, and expectation ran through them both. "I'm going to kiss you here now, *Mon Amour*."

Her eyes widened, and he settled between her legs. His first taste of her was heaven itself. She opened for him like a flower, giving him what they both craved.

He laved her cunny with his tongue, taunting her little nubbin. She tasted as sweet as wine. Her hips swayed against his mouth, and he suckled harder, teased her relentlessly.

She moaned his name, her fingers spiking into his hair and holding him against her. He could feel that she was close, the seductive dance of her body as her orgasm grew was telling, and he concentrated, wanting her to come at the behest of his mouth.

He did not have to wait long. She pushed against him, gasped his name, and rocked against his lips through her pleasure. Her legs shook as her orgasm ripped through her every extremity. That they were far from anyone to hear, he reveled in the sound and the fact he had made her reach her pleasure.

He settled her shift back down her legs and came to lay beside her, watching her slowly return to earth. "Are you pleased, my love?" he asked

She stared at the ceiling before meeting his eyes. "More than pleased. That was utterly breathtaking."

"Wait until we're together fully, and I make you come, my love. Now that will be extraordinary."

Her eyes widened, and wonder washed over her features. "I hope to find out one day. More than anything in the world."

"You will," he stated. "But now you must eat. Come," he said, sitting up and pulling her along with him. "The day is young, but we only have a stolen amount of time before I have to return you to London. The opera followed by Lord and Lady Craig's ball is this evening, and I need us both to attend."

"Really?" She followed him over to the small table, throwing him an amused grin when he helped her to sit before stealing a quick kiss. "Why?" she asked.

"Because it is only events like those, and this one, when I can steal you away and spend time with you, as scandalous as that is. And there are already too many hours between now and this evening before we meet again."

She picked up a small sandwich and bit into the soft bread. "Are you saying you will miss me, Lord Billington?"

He poured them both a cup of tea. "I fear I shall miss you even when you are my wife."

SIXTEEN

K nox arrived at the opera and was pleased to find Miss York was already there with the Duke and Duchess of Derby by her side. They stood talking with other members of their set in the foyer of the Theatre Royal, and for a moment he stood, watching her, admiring the view that was his intended.

Their morning together at his small estate, the enjoyment it wrought within him, was something he had never experienced before. The emotions that rioted within him whenever they were around each other were not common and ought to be savored and protected.

How thankful he was that Lord Collins had caught them in the library at his lordship's ball.

"Billington," Derby stated, shaking his hand. "It is good of you to come." He excused them from the party to speak a moment privately. "If you wish to sit with Miss York, you may have the two seats at the back of our box. Maybe join us this evening instead of sitting in your booth. It will make for a more enjoyable performance if you're with your intended," he suggested.

Knox was more than willing to join them. "Thank you for the invitation. I shall do as you ask." And take advantage of being near Miss York. After their day at his small country estate, he had thought of nothing but her. Of being near her again, stealing a touch or two, maybe even a kiss.

Miss York met his eyes across the room and he could not look away. His body yearned to be near her again. Surprisingly, he did not go up in flames, so warm were his thoughts of her.

She sauntered over to him, a mischievous smile on her kissable lips. "Lord Billington. You're to join our small party this evening. How very fortunate we are," she said.

He breathed deep the scent of jasmine that always accompanied her. "I've missed you since we parted earlier today. I hope you're not too tired from our exertions."

"Not at all. If anything, I'm invigorated by the jaunt." Her seductive chuckle almost made him whisk her into a nearby vacant room and show her more of what he could do to her. What she could do to him.

"You're mischievous and so damn alluring you make me ache," he whispered against her ear.

He felt her shiver beside him, and he brushed his hand against hers, wishing he could hold it and never let it go.

She licked her lips, and his cock twitched. "We are to sit beside each other for the performance. I'm looking forward to the evening even more now," she said as the duchess hurried them along to join them as they made their way upstairs.

Without thought, Miss York entwined her arm with his as they followed their group. Knox reveled in the feel of her beside him, wanting her there now and always.

They came to the box, and he pulled her close as everyone took their seats before they did the same. Their position in the box afforded them more privacy than the other seats. Here they were shadowed by the walls of the theater, and although they could still see the stage well enough, there were so many before them that they could talk without causing offense.

"You look beautiful this evening, Miss York," he said, wanting to compliment her so upon seeing her again.

A blush stole across her cheeks, and he could see she was trying not to grin. "You like my gown?" she asked him, slipping her hand across the top of her bodice and bringing his attention to follow her finger as it slipped along the tops of her breasts.

He clamped his mouth shut and fought for restraint. He leaned toward her, his lips brushing the lobe of her ear. "I would like your gown even more, should it be about your ankles."

Her mouth opened with a small gasp before wickedness flickered in her eyes. "My Lord Billington, how naughty. Almost as deviant as your mouth was on me today." She met his eyes, and he read the need burning bright in their green depths. "I want your mouth on me again," she whispered.

They were so close that should they be looked upon, it would almost seem as if they were being intimate. He pulled back and fought not to drag her from the box. The music to the opera began, but he heard very little. His heart thumped loudly in his ears, and he fought to think of how to remove her from here. To have her alone so he could give her what she wanted.

Hell, what they both wanted.

Miss York leaned forward and whispered something in the Duchess of Derby's ear. The duchess nodded and smiled at her friend before Miss York stood and left the box.

Knox hesitated all but a moment before he went after her. He hoped no one noticed from their set, but he also did not care. He caught sight of Miss York slipping into the women's retiring room, and for a moment, he debated what he should do. Perhaps her leaving had been for legitimate reasons, and his following her was reprehensible.

He moved into a vacant room, stood beside a window, and watched the London traffic pass before the theater before slippered feet sounded on the passage outside. He cleared his throat as Miss York passed the room on her way back to watch the show. She glanced toward the sound and, upon spying him, entered and closed the door.

"I thought you may follow me," she admitted, the snick of the lock loud in his ears. A knell that ignited his need, a wildness that would not be sated.

He strode over to her and kissed her. Hard. Their mouths fused and fought for control. Their tongues tangled, their bodies ground against the other.

"Let me have you," he gasped against her lips.

Lila pressed a finger against his lips and shook her head. "Not here, not this night. But there is something you can allow me to do," she said, a mischievous turn to her lips.

"Anything," he said, his body almost beyond his control.

"Let me give you pleasure."

Her words made his knees weak, and he leaned against a nearby desk, watching her, debating if he had heard her right. "You cannot be serious?" he asked for clarification.

She sauntered over to him, settling on her knees. "Oh, I'm serious, my lord."

NEVER IN HER LIFE HAD SHE EVER ACTED so shameless. A woman who asked for what she wanted and demanded nothing but her desires be agreed to. Her mouth watered at the thought of doing what he did to her today, and she was certain it must be possible. In some manner, in any case.

His eyes burned with fire, his breathing ragged. He clasped his falls and tore them open, slipping his hand into his breeches and pulling out his sizable manhood.

It jutted before her eyes, and she took in all his glory. How marvelous he was, the veins engorged and running up his length. A little bead of moisture settled on his manhood, and she leaned forward, licking it. It was salty but not unlikeable.

"Bloody hell," he cursed, his hand slipping about her neck.

"I'm going to taste you again, Billington," she said, determined to get her way.

He nodded but did not dispute her. "Knox. You're about to have my cock in your mouth. You cannot call me Billington."

She chuckled and covered his manhood with her lips. He was large, her mouth stretching, and she suckled him, laving him with her tongue and teasing him. He squirmed under her, his hand flexing on her neck, his hips thrusting and pushing him farther down her throat.

She sucked him as hard as she could, wanting him to find the pleasure she had experienced earlier that day. He had been hard, ready for release when he had kissed her mons, and had there been more time, she would have given him as much joy as he had bestowed on her.

But there had not been. Now, however, they were at the opera, the *ton* occupied by the performance on the stage, and she could concentrate on giving him what they both wanted.

Pleasure.

"*Mon Amour*," he groaned, thrusting into her mouth. "You're going to make me spend."

"Hmm," she moaned, and he cursed a second time before he wrenched out of her mouth and brought her to stand before him.

Lila stared at him. "What is wrong? Do you not like what I'm doing?" she asked him.

He picked her up and set her on the small table, pushing her to lie back on the wood. "My turn," he said.

"But I haven't made you reach your pleasure," she argued.

"This will give me enough pleasure."

Lila sat up, clasping his shirt in her fist. "No, I want you to come too," she said. "Is there a way that can be achieved without losing my virginity?" she asked.

He closed his eyes, a muscle working in his jaw. "There is what we did in the carriage, if you remember. But I want you so much more now. I do not know if I can control myself."

"You will hold your restraint," she reasoned. "Do it, Knox," she cooed. "Do it again."

He hoisted her legs about his hips and pressed against her. His hard manhood and soft, velvety skin slipped against hers with ease, and she bit back a moan as he pressed and teased her sex.

She clasped his shoulders, fighting back the need to moan his name. "Knox," she whispered, grinding as best she could against him.

"I know, my love. I know," he said, his whispered words against her ear making her shiver.

This was too delicious for words. Never had she wanted him to take her as much as she did right at this moment. He pressed and slipped their bodies together. Made for one another. Tension coiled to a breaking point within her, and she knotted her feet together about his back, their bodies all but one as he continued to tease them relentlessly.

"I'm going to come," he groaned.

She took his lips and kissed him, and he swallowed her gasp, her moan of pleasure as her release rocked through her. Every inch of her body came alive, tingled, and pulsated. It was too much and yet, never enough.

He would never be enough, and she would always want more. Of him, of this. Of everything he could give her.

"*Mon Amour*, you undo me."

She bit her lip, wishing he knew her name, and wanting to hear him say her name now and forever. "As do you me," she said, hoping this night could last forever, that they could stay co-cooned from the *ton* for a little while longer.

But knowing they could not.

SEVENTEEN

The following morning Lila pushed her horse at breakneck speed along Rotten Row, heedless of the no-galloping rule that the park enforced. No one was about at this time, and she needed to run free, feel the wind in her hair, the thud of the horse's hooves drumming in her ears.

She was a terrible person, and today she would have to tell the man she loved that she had been lying to him.

Being intimate with him when all along he believed her to be someone else... As much as she had hoped he would know the difference between her and Harlow, he had not, and she could not fool herself or him anymore regarding the matter.

He deserved the truth and to decide what would happen between them next, no matter if that meant she was ruined forever. After playing such games with him, she would deserve nothing less.

"Miss York."

The sound of her name echoing across the park was surely a figment of her imagination. Brought on by her need to see Lord Billington. To say she was sorry for the mess she had set in motion. A motion that her sister had foolishly suggested, but she had agreed to. And now she was doomed.

"Harlow!"

Her sister's name was like a stab to her heart. Lila tightened the reins, trying to pull up her horse. Her mare slowed into a trot and eventually a walk. Lila halted near a copse of trees and shifted in the saddle to look behind her. She felt her eyes widen at the sight of Lord Billington cantering toward her, his dark hair flying about his glorious visage in the crisp morning air. His cravat hung loose about his neck.

His smile made the morning a little brighter, and she wished things could be different between them. But they could not be.

Her deception had gone far enough, and it had to stop. He deserved the truth. Last evening she had almost given herself to him, a step neither of them could take back. She could not allow that to happen again.

"Lord Billington, I did not think you or anyone else was in the park so early," she said.

His attention slid over her like a caress, and she shivered. One brow rose disbelievingly before he said, "Astride, Miss York. You are pushing the boundaries today, along with your galloping," he teased.

She shrugged. The nerves in her belly told her the lie was something she could no longer live with. Not anymore. He deserved to know the truth before they married, and she had to tell him her true identity before the priest's presence.

Oh dear lord, her time here in London had become a disaster.

"I wished to ride astride this morning," she stated, looking to ensure they were still alone before she said what she must. "I cannot marry you, Lord Billington," she blurted, needing to state such a fact before another moment passed.

He started at her words before a frown deepened between his brow. "Let me assure you, Miss York, you will. We have been caught in a compromising position that we both enjoyed. Quite a lot, I might add. While it is not how I wanted you to agree to marry me, it is the reason why it will happen."

She shook her head, not willing to relent. "I'm not who you think I am. I'm not Harlow as you believe."

His horse stomped his front hoof, sensing Lord Billington's change in emotion. "I beg your pardon. Whatever are you talking about?" he asked her.

Lila took a calming breath. It was time he knew the truth. "I've been lying to you, my lord. My sister Harlow whom you had been courting, returned home. She begged me to return to town and be the one to deny you her hand as she was unable to stomach such a duty. She could not do it herself, you see. She's never been good with conflict, and I tried to tell you that I could not marry you, but you would not listen to me, and now we've been caught, and I do not know what to do."

His mouth gaped before he looked past her, his mind clearly reeling at what she said.

Had she shocked him mute?

"We look so alike, you see," she continued. "Harlow believed you would not be able to tell the difference, and you did not. But then, I have always admired you, thought well of you, and," she shrugged, "I fell in love. I have never been courted before, so when you asked for the chance to change my mind, I did not think there was any harm. I thought we would spend some weeks becoming good friends, but that is all, before I returned home to Grafton. No harm would come to you by my choice not to marry you. But then we kissed, and then we kissed again, and we were caught, and now..." Lila did not know what else to say. No words of apology were strong enough to say so that he would forgive what she had done to him.

"You're not Harlow?" he scoffed and released a little manic laugh that made her cringe.

"No. I'm not Harlow. I'm Lila, the eldest sister. The one you showed no interest in years ago when I had my two Seasons."

KNOX CRINGED AT THE BARB MISS YORK delivered, but she was mistaken if she thought he would forgive her or take any blame for this cruel hoax.

What kind of people were these Grafton folks to trick a lord of the realm? A viscount and future duke. Were they mad?

"How dare you play along with such an absurd scheme. You ought to know better, as your sister should." He ran a hand through his hair, unable to comprehend she had swung him a merry dance. "And you're Miss Lila York, you mentioned." He studied the woman before him, and the truth of her words started to penetrate his mind. Her eyes were a fiercer green and more almond-shaped than what he remembered. Not to mention her hair, a darker shade of brown that shimmered with golden highlights in the breaking dawn.

"The mole," he exclaimed. "It's on the opposite side of your face." He shook his head, watching her in disbelief. "I cannot believe I did not realize that fact sooner. How blind I have been."

He stared at her, unable to hide the loathing and disgust he felt at this betrayal. This was the York sisters' fault, and he had a right to be angry and upset. If Miss York expected a different reaction from him than the one she was receiving, she would be sadly mistaken.

"I'm sorry, my lord. I thought we would be friends, and then I would leave. I did not think we would...that I would allow..."

"That we would kiss? That you would allow me to hold you as I did, touch you. God damn it, Lila. I had my mouth between your legs. You've had my cock in yours!" He ran a hand over his mouth, his eyes wide with horror. "And all the while, I was kissing a woman who was not who I thought she was. This is beyond forgivable."

"I'm sorry," she pleaded. "You were never meant to find out, and I know," she quickly added, holding up her hand to stop another tirade from spilling from his lips, "you do not wish to hear any excuses, but my sister said you would not listen to her. That she had tried to show you without hurting your feelings that she did not welcome your suit, and you would not relent."

"Oh," he blustered. "So this is my fault now. Are you saying, madam, that I was forcing myself on her? That I pressed my suit when it was not welcome?"

She raised her chin defiantly. "Can you deny it? Was she not cool toward your advances? Should you not have picked up on her clues?"

"And yet you returned and gave me hope. I thought a changed personality and fresh outlook on our union's possibility. But then, it was not Harlow York who had this sudden transformation. It was her spinster sister desperate for a husband and frantic to enjoy a little pet here and kiss there before she scuttled back to Grafton."

Lila gasped, glaring at him. "How dare you speak to me like that. I grant you the right to be angry, but you do not have to be cruel."

A muscle worked in his jaw, and he tore his gaze from her, staring between his horse's ears. He could not believe her words. They were too fanciful and absurd. "This union, this farce of an engagement, is over, madam. I will not marry a liar or a woman who is not even the one I had chosen to be my bride. You may go to the devil for all I care."

"Well, I believe I stated that I would not marry you first, so do keep up, Lord Billington." Lila turned her mount around and clicked her tongue. She pushed her horse forward and left him alone in the park.

Knox shut his eyes as despair encircled his heart. This was not what he had expected upon finding her at the park this morning. How had everything that seemed right and good turn into something wrong and bad?

He thought he loved the woman cantering away from him, but in truth, he did not know who that woman was at all.

Eighteen

Knox downed another brandy, having lost count after his fifth, or was it his sixth? His friend—and the only man he was comfortable with telling his sad, ridiculous tale to—Renford sat across from him. However, the duke was more sedate than he and still on his first brandy.

"The chit has been lying to me. They were playing me the fool the entire time. I kissed her. The wrong sister," he blurted his words, not a little slurred. Damn it. He had done a lot more than kiss the chit. They had almost fucked numerous times, not to mention other things... "Who does such a thing to another?" He shook his head, unable to comprehend still several hours after their confrontation in the park.

He pushed aside the hurt that had sparked in her eyes at his lowly remark of her spinsterhood.

Miss Lila York. He recalled her. Well, he sort

of remembered her. He sighed. Who was he fooling? He did not recollect her really at all. The year of her debut had been one that he had been busy trying to secure his first mistress, and securing a wife was the last thing on his mind.

A typical lad, new to town and ready to be free, to enjoy adventure, sex, and fun.

There was nothing wrong with that. Every young man began his time in town in such ways. It was not his fault he had not noticed her.

"It seems the York sisters do," Renford drawled. "But you know, my good man, you do need to marry her. Or at least force the union upon the other sister now that you have kissed her and been caught. No matter how much you may not want to, I know you would not allow her to suffer the consequences of your actions."

Knox glared at the golden liquid in his tumbler. Damn his friend for the truth of his words. No, he could not allow her to suffer a ruined reputation, not when he had been the one who had clutched at her, devoured her soft, tempting lips in that library. Or tasted other sweet lips that made his cock twitch.

He growled. "Damn it all to hell. I ought to marry Harlow just to spite Lila York and her wicked temptations."

Renford snorted. "Oh, do tell. That sounds like a promising beginning to a marriage if you ask me," he said. "But," he shrugged, "what do I know? I'm possibly the last person you ought to be seeking advice from."

Knox doubted that. Renford had always had a good, sound character and did not lie or fluff about with the truth. Unlike some people whom he had the unfortunate event of meeting this Season and wanting as his wife.

"So you're telling me that I have to speak to Miss Lila York and explain to her that my gentlemanly ideals will not allow me to break the engagement and that she is to plan for a wedding for as soon as it may be."

"That is what I'm suggesting, and settle it all tonight if you can manage to sober up quick enough. The York sisters tend to flee London when they do not wish to face a troublesome problem. After this evening, she may leave London. She may have already left," Renford suggested.

Knox met Renford's gaze at his words, the unwelcome knot in his gut more troubling than the idea of marrying a lying chit. He loathed liars and people who manipulated to get their way. That he was now forced to marry one because he could not allow her to take the fall for them both was annoying as hell.

"So I'm to marry the elder Miss York. What will society think? They will know some foolery has been played and will not act kindly."

"That is true," Renford agreed, standing and

placing his empty tumbler on the mantel. "The question is how you will go on with the elder Miss York. Were you so in love with the younger sibling that to marry the older is beyond anything you can stomach?"

Knox downed his brandy, and the room spun a little quicker. "No, I never loved the younger Miss York, even if they are practically identical. But the trick they have played upon me is unforgivable. I shall marry her, but that is all." That Miss York knew his dislike of liars and still, all the while, was taking part in one of the biggest lying schemes he had ever heard of in London was more than he could tolerate.

"She will want children. What will you do then?" Renford asked, one curious brow raised.

Knox beat down the lick of desire those words ignited in him at the thought of bedding Miss Lila York. She was a beautiful woman with a body worth savoring and worshipping. What a shame her mouth was as poisonous as a snake.

"I will do my husbandly duties, but there will be nothing between us. She has broken my trust; once such a bond is broken, it cannot be rebuilt. A leopard does not change his spots after all."

"She may prove you wrong, Billington."

Knox closed his eyes, sleep pulling at his body. "I doubt that," he said before a welcoming blackness engulfed him.

· · ·

LILA COULD NOT STAND ANY MORE compliments and congratulations on her impending marriage to Viscount Billington. She had not been at Lady Hirch's ball for more than an hour, and yet that was all she had been spoken to about. All that anyone wanted to hear.

Details. Details. Details.

Particulars she did not know herself and possibly never would. Not now that Billington had told her that he would not be marrying her at all. That she could go to the devil for all he cared.

Not that he had delivered those last thoughts, but she could read between his anger and knew he was upset. He had a right to be, of course, and after this evening, she would leave London and hide forever in Grafton.

She would explain the terrible situation to her sister, and Harlow could come to London, break the engagement and move on with her life. Most of this mess could be laid at Harlow's feet, and Lila would not continue being the target of all Billington's ire. She hoped not to see that man ever again.

Liar.

She sighed. Was he furious enough to do something foolish, like proclaim aloud the wicked plan Harlow had come up with for all the *ton* to hear, ruining their reputations forever?

The Duchess of Derby stood beside her, and she listened to the conversation surrounding her.

Talk of the married ladies' weddings. What they suggested she offer to her guests at the breakfast. Asking questions about where they would travel for their honeymoon.

All things that Lila knew would never come to pass and something she need not concern herself with.

She supposed when she left London, and the truth came out, as it always had a way of doing, she would see even less of her good friend Hailey.

If only she could travel back in time and repair the damage her actions had caused. Her friendship with the duchess was one she held most dear in life, and to know that her actions would now make it even more impossible for them to see each other made her heart ache.

"Oh, and here he comes now. The besotted Lord Billington," Lady Hirch tittered, smiling toward his lordship.

Lila turned and felt the blood drain from her face. Billington strode toward her with purposeful steps, but his face held not one ounce of pleasure as it once had. Now it was all hard lines, a severe frown between his brows, and his eyes cold as ice.

She blinked back tears knowing, how much he must loathe her now, and she was about to find out just how much. So too would the *ton* circling them, who she was sure were about to hear the truth.

"Lord Billington," Lady Derby said, coming to stand closer to Lila as if she could too feel the tension radiating off the viscount.

"My lord," Lila said, dipping into a curtsy and glad her moment of looking at the floor gave her some respite from his hostility.

"Your Grace, Miss York, a pleasure as always." He turned to the other ladies present and his lips lifted into a small, charming smile. "Ladies, a delight also," he said.

Lila ignored the captivated sighs that surrounded her as his alluring voice paid the compliment. She met his eyes and waited for the axe he no doubt held to swing and cut off her head. "Good evening," she said at last.

He clasped her hand and placed it on his arm, covering her hand with his. "I hope you're all busy discussing our upcoming nuptials. Lady Hirch," he said, singling out the middle-aged widow. "I'm sure you can give my darling wife-to-be some ideas on how a wedding of true charm and beauty can be achieved."

Lila gaped at Billington, not believing what he was saying. It sounded as though he was going to marry her after all. Or was he going to marry Harlow and have her pretend to be his betrothed until then?

The thought made her stomach heave, and she took a calming breath, unwilling to say anything here and now just in case her worst nightmare was about to come true.

Where she would see the man she had always coveted marry her sister instead of herself. Where she would have to stand aside and watch her only chance of happiness promise himself to someone else.

Not just for here and now, but forever.

NINETEEN

Lila swallowed the bile that rose in her throat and pulled from Lord Billington. "If you'll excuse me a moment. I shall be back directly," she explained to everyone, starting for the ballroom doors and the direction the retiring room was located this evening.

She made it to the first floor of Lady Hirch's town house before Billington slipped his hand around the top of her arm and started her in the opposite direction to where she wanted to go.

"What are you doing?" she demanded, trying to pull her arm from his. "I require the retiring room," she lied, having known she was only going to sit in there and while away several minutes where she would not have to see anyone or discuss any more of a wedding the man at her side did not want.

"We need to talk," was all he said before he whisked her into a dark bedroom. The curtains were open, moonlight their only source of light, and even then, it was lacking as the moon had not yet risen to its full height.

"We have nothing to discuss at all, my lord. You have made your wishes clear. In fact," she said, finally freeing herself from his hold and crossing her arms. "Why would you lie like that downstairs just now? You said you would not marry me, and while I do not blame you for that, lying is something you dislike, is it not? Mayhap you ought not to be doing it then?" she scolded. Anger thrummed through her at the whole situation, not just what she had done but how he had spoken to her as if she were not worthy of love.

A desperate spinster as he so termed her. Was that not what he hurled in her face but yesterday?

"We need to discuss how we will move forward after this debacle. After much thought and discussion with a friend who is seeing things more clearly than I am at this present time, he has made me see that I cannot cry off from this wedding. We were seen in a comprising position and will have to marry. I think it is best that we have a quiet, small wedding, family only, so we limit the scandal of who exactly I'm marrying rather than who the *ton* believes I'm to wed."

Lila strode to the window, staring out over the inky-black gardens. "I'm sure I can speak to my sister, and in time maybe she will see that marrying you is what she wants after all. I should so hate to upset the *ton* and let them talk of you marrying the over-the-hill matron spinster from Grafton instead of the Season's diamond Harlow York."

He watched her, and she could see a muscle in his jaw flex at her words. "I was angry and upset yesterday, shocked to my core, and said things I did not mean."

Lila shook her head, walking toward him. "No, that is where you're wrong, my lord. When one is angry, one says the truth more than anything else. You do not love me, and you certainly do not like me at present. Scandal or not, I think this union is a bad idea, and I cannot marry you."

Lila brushed past him and hoped he would not try to stop her. He did not, and she strolled into the passage, the sound of Billington's footsteps soon hard on her heels before Lady Hirch stepped out of the retiring room farther along and spied them both.

"Billington, Miss York, you are not married yet," she chided, meeting them at the stairs. "But do not fret, my dears. Since you're to be married within a few weeks, I shall not say a word to anyone. I will, however, tell you how much we're looking forward to seeing one of London's most delightful debutantes and a renowned bachelor joined together in marriage. Oh, what a satisfying day that will be," she said, clapping her hands together in glee.

Lila nodded, forcing a smile on her lips when all she really wished to do was scream. "Thank you, Lady Hirch. We, too, are very much looking forward to our day."

"Of course you are, my dear," she said before starting down the stairs.

"See," Billington whispered in her ear, sending a frisson of desire down her spine. "We have no choice."

"If you stopped dragging me into rooms alone and then only to be caught, we would have a choice," she spat back at him.

"From what I recall, you were only too happy to be alone with me when it suited, or was all that you stated lies along with who you were portraying?"

Lila studied him, wondering why he even cared to know. "I lied because my sister was desperate and in need of help. But otherwise, Lord Billington, I do not lie. It is not my usual penchant."

"We will marry and have to endure it as best we can."

"I do not want my marriage to be endured. What kind of life is that? I want my husband to want me, to love me, not to tolerate me. And I certainly do not want a husband who is in love with my sister."

"We have no choice, madam."

"Do you intend to lie with me? Will you consummate the marriage? Will you be willing to have children? Tell me, so I know what I shall do."

"I will do my duty as a gentleman, and I would not have been looking for a wife had I not wanted children. You shall have all of those things, but that is all."

Could she tolerate such a union for the rest of her life? Could she give up the hope of finding a love match, not that she had not given up such a dream years ago, to have a marriage? He would give her children.

Marriage would mean she would have her own home, freedom that came to a woman of rank and fortune. No longer a spinster, but a wife, even if one in name only.

"Very well, Billington, I shall marry you under those conditions, but I want children as soon as possible. I'm old, as you know. Six and twenty, and my teeth may soon fall out. So as decrepit as I am, we do not want to scare our children when they look upon me, now do we?"

He stared at her, his attention dipping to her lips when she mentioned her teeth. "Ah, no, we do not." He took a deep breath and nodded. "Very good then. We have come to an agreement. I shall call on you tomorrow, and we shall discuss the particulars with your aunt, and I would suggest you write to your parents and your devious sister and have them return to town. There is much to do."

He did not wait for her, merely started down the stairs and out the front door, not bothering to reenter the ball. She shook her head. Well, it would seem she was not going to be dancing any time soon with her betrothed.

She ought to have negotiated that as well into their agreement. She would hate not to dance with him again, not that she didn't deserve the treatment she was receiving. She earned his anger wholeheartedly.

THE FOLLOWING AFTERNOON KNOX kicked his heels in the yellow parlor of Lila's aunt's London home. The room was overly bright and a little too gaudy for his taste, but then he was a man and preferred greens and blues to light, pastel colors.

The door opened, and in strolled his future wife. Miss Lila York was dressed in a morning gown of green muslin, and her eyes shone as bright as a jade gem.

He beat down his pulse that kicked up a notch at the sight of her. He would not desire his wife, not after she had pretended to be someone else merely to throw him off when it suited her.

But he could not deny that he was marrying

one of England's prettiest, most intelligent chits. Devious too.

She came toward him, and he was reminded of how tall she was and what a perfect height she was to suit him. He schooled his features to one of disinterest and boredom and bowed. "Miss York, thank you for allowing me to wait fifteen minutes before you decided to grace me with your presence."

"You are very welcome," she said, her smile as equally false as his attempt at civility. "I had hoped that you would have grown bored by waiting so long and left. But it would seem luck is not with me today." She flopped onto a nearby settee with little finesse and settled her skirts about her legs.

He sat across from her, forcing himself to let go of her barb. He needed to get on with the organizing of this wedding they were to endure. "I thought we should get married in the church on my York estate. By using the location to our advantage, we can vet who's invited and who is not. Just as we ought to do, considering the vicar will be announcing a Miss Lila York to take my hand and not one Miss Harlow York instead."

Her eyes narrowed, and he could see she was angry at his reminding her of such a fact.

"Would your family be willing to travel to York, do you think?"

"Of course they would," she said, her expression pinched. "But perhaps you would like me to talk to Harlow, see if there is any way that she may prefer you after all."

"No," he barked, standing to pace before the line of windows that overlooked the backyard. "That will not be necessary. She fled London to avoid a marriage proposal. I think that it is clear enough her emotions were not engaged."

"But yours were, my lord. Marrying you feels wrong. I have thought about it since last evening, and I do not want to marry you when you're in love with my sister. It makes my stomach recoil."

He stared at her, wondering why she would have that emotional response to what they were embarking on. "I did not love your sister. She was the diamond of the Season, and I needed a wife. The match seemed suitable for me, nothing more than that."

His betrothed's face blanched. "Somehow, I feel your answer as to why you wished to marry Harlow is worse."

"And now, thanks to your untruths, you will suffer such a fate instead," he quipped, his stomach recoiling at the thought.

What a stupendous match they were.

TWENTY

Lila sat and listened, not adding too much to all to Lord Billington's ideas and plans for their upcoming wedding. There was little she could do about it all. Her aunt had written to her family and asked them to join her in London before she had a chance to delay the news.

She supposed they would all be in town in the next week, and she would have to face Harlow. Her poor sister would not understand the mess she made here in town.

"The next matter we must discuss is how we go about town until we leave. We must put on a show for the *ton* and make society believe we're a love match. I dislike gossip, as you know, and do not want to be the focus of tattletale lies about town, so we need to discuss how we shall carry on."

"In what way?" Lila frowned, unsure of what he meant and not sure she wanted to know.

He came and sat beside her. His presence overwhelmed her senses and reminded her of all the delicious times they were alone. Such as they were now. She swallowed, her attention settling on his lips. Lips now pressed into a thin, displeased line before he disclosed his plan.

"We must fool the *ton* into believing that we're a love match. When they find out that I married Miss Lila York instead of Harlow, whom they all believed was in town and whom I was courting, it may help if they believe we fell in love instead."

"I thought we had, but never mind, all of those declarations seem to be in error too." She folded her hands in her lap to stop their shaking. "You want us to act as if we cannot tolerate being apart? Have us both be near one another at every ball and event?" She inwardly groaned. She had hoped to leave today back to Grafton and stop her parents from traveling to town, but she knew that was no longer an option.

"I do not think we should continue this farce. We are only making matters worse for both of us," she said.

Or at least worst for her. She loved Knox with all her heart, that he had only denied loving Harlow and had not mentioned the emotion between them since finding out the truth told her he may not feel the same.

"It is better than the alternative," he stated. "The sooner the *ton* believes we're a love match and that I fell in love with Lila York and not your sister, the sooner we can return to normal in our otherwise muddy lives. I will sacrifice my dislike of lying this one time if it means someone else will be the *ton's* fodder for gossip."

Lila pushed up from the settee, sick to death, hearing what she was. "Enough, Billington. All you do is worry about what everyone else thinks of you and is saying behind your back. Is it not exhausting?"

His stare made her feel like a child. "You will do this because you and your sister are the reason we are marrying at all. The sooner we fool the *ton*, the sooner we can stop pretending so hard to love one another and merely fade into oblivion and return to our normal lives. Even though we will forever be joined in holy matrimony."

"Do not remind me," she quipped, disliking the idea more and more of being his wife. "So we will dance and flirt, and will you be bestowing upon me any more kisses, my lord? I would like to prepare myself if you're to go beyond your endurance and bestow such a blessing on me."

His eyes narrowed. "Do not pretend that you did not like my kisses, Lila," he said, using her given name for the first time, leaving her skin to prickle in awareness. "You kissed me back, so I'm sure should I choose for us to be caught yet again kissing at an event, you will not complain."

The audacity of the man had no bounds. "And if I do not want to be kissed by you? What then, you will force me into the act?" she asked.

He blanched. "Of course not, but we need to beat down the scandal that's about to engulf all of London when they find out I married you instead of your sister."

"I do not care what they think, and I refuse to do as you say." Lila knew she was being churlish, but she could not help it. As much as she wanted to kiss Billington again, to kiss him as a means to please the *ton* was not ideal. To pretend that she adored him when a little part of her wanted that to be true, hurt.

"Fine, we shall not kiss, but you will pretend to be happy about this situation, especially since it is your doing."

"Oh dear lord, please stop reminding me."

KNOX FUMBLED TO FIND THE RIGHT words to reply to Lila. Was the chit mad? Did she not know in what a precarious situation they now sat? The *ton* could make or break a family and their connections to everything. He did not want his future children injured by this scandal that would forever be held over their heads.

"Think of our children. They do not want to enter society or be ostracized because of a scandal that touched their parents twenty years before. You said you wanted children, did you not?" he said. Not that he wanted to bribe her into cooperation, but he would do what he had to.

The woman was maddening and utterly delectable when in high color and annoyed at him as she was. She had spunk, he would give her that, and he liked that she would argue with him, not merely allow him to get his own way.

Even though he would in this, it showed she at least had a backbone.

"Fine, I shall kiss you and pretend to worship the ground you walk on, does that suit?" she asked, her words sweet, but her mocking visage told him she was less than pleased about it all.

"Very good, now we shall practice." Her shocked gasp sounded loud in the room, and he almost laughed.

"Now, what is the point of kissing here? There is no one to see or catch us. My aunt will not, not now that we're betrothed."

"It must look genuine, not forced."

She wagged one finger before his face. "But it's all of those things. How will it look anything but that?" She stood and walked to the window.

She had a point. Still, they needed to do this. He followed her. "Kiss me as you have before, and

I will tell you if we will be able to fool the *ton* when we return to society as a married couple."

She placed her hands on her hips. "Why do you not kiss me instead? This is your idea, after all."

"Fine," he said, exasperated. Without waiting for her to argue the point further, he clasped her cheeks and closed the space between them. The blush of annoyance made her inherently pretty, and little emerald shards of color burned with annoyance in her eyes.

He beat down the urge to compliment her on how damn enchanting she was and took her mouth instead.

His body shuddered at their first kiss since her betrayal. He wasn't sure what came over him, annoyance, anger, lust, but damn it all to hell, a little part of him, deep down and buried, wanted her again.

Even knowing all that he did of her. What she had done. The tricks she played.

He craved her.

He stroked her tongue with his, and she relaxed in his arms. Her face tipped up to better suit the embrace, and he slid his hands into her hair. Pins and curls fell about her shoulders. He wanted to see her disheveled but did not dare break the kiss.

Her mouth sought his, her tongue tentative at first, but soon stroked his with an inquisitiveness that sent his blood to pump fast and hot in his veins.

He walked her back and did not stop until she came up against the wall beside the window. She let out a little moan as his body came into contact with hers.

She was all warm lines and womanly curves. His hand slipped over her hip, pulling her closer as he pressed into her. His cock ached and stood to attention. Heat licked his spine, and he knew pretending to be in lust with the woman in his arms would be no chore.

Never had he felt this way. Not even with her sister, whom he never had once wanted to kiss.

Why was that when they were practically identical?

Because Lila makes you feel things you never did before, it's not material but an emotional difference.

Even if the woman had lured him to her heat with lies and deceit, he was lost.

TWENTY-ONE

To kiss Billington again was like everything that had gone wrong with her life had turned around and disappeared. The troubles she had caused were somehow all forgotten, and he wanted her after all.

All lies, of course. He despised her now, and even though they were to be married, it would take a long time, if not forever, to get him to trust and love her as he once had.

If he ever loved her at all. He had thought she was Harlow...

But here and now, kissing him and feeling dizzy with desire, with hope, she could not help but imagine through such intimacy, she may have a way of reaching his heart and making him forgive her.

She had only been trying to help her sister.

Surely that was not so bad and worthy of hatred for the rest of her life.

He wrenched her out of his hold, and she stumbled, feeling the severing like a cut to her heart. "That will do very well. I'm sure we can fool the *ton* that we're a love match when we return a married couple."

"And will it fool them regarding my identity? Or have you forgotten who I am?" she asked, ice all but dripping from her tone.

He narrowed his eyes, striding over to a nearby sideboard and pouring himself a whisky. "We will pretend that they were mistaken all along. That you both were in town, and people merely became confused as to who I was courting. They cannot prove otherwise. You are so very similar."

"So I suppose it would not matter to you whom you kissed. Your reaction would be the same whether it was my sister or me. Is that what you're saying?" He could hurt her, and he possibly would with his answer, but she had to know if she was different from Harlow. That somewhere deep in his soul, he recognized his soul mate, and the fire and attraction they had shared had arrived from that.

"I never kissed your sister, so I cannot say." He drank down his whisky and strode toward the door. "I shall see you at Lord and Lady Daniels' ball this evening. My carriage will collect you at nine sharp. Do not keep me waiting."

Lila watched him leave. He did not look back once. How he must despise her, even if his kisses were so very wicked.

And now, in a matter of days, she would have her sister and parents in town, and her interactions with Billington were sure to be more awkward than before.

How would he be before her sibling?

She supposed she would soon find out.

KNOX COULD NOT LEAVE LILA'S HOME any quicker without actually breaking out into a run and looking like a foolish idiot for doing so. He climbed up into his carriage and ordered his driver to Whites.

A good, stiff drink and the absence of women were just what he needed.

He leaned back in the squabs, his mind a whirl of thoughts and emotions. He closed his eyes and tried to form a coherent thought, but all he could think of was the kiss he had shared with Lila.

She drove him to the brink of desperation, and yet never had he ever been so enraged at a single person in his life.

The carriage rocked several minutes later to a halt, and he jumped down without waiting for the Whites footman to open the carriage door. Upon entering the establishment, he climbed the stairs two at a time and made his way to his favorite location beside the windows that overlooked St. James Street.

A footman took his order, and Knox closed his eyes, reveling in the solitude of the room at this time in the afternoon.

"Oh no, I know that look. What has happened?" His good friend Renford quipped before the squeak of leather sounded loud in his ears as he sat.

"Nothing is the matter besides the fact that I'm going to be the laughing idiot of London and all thanks to me not knowing that the woman I've been trying to court is not the same woman I thought she was at all."

Renford listened with a considerate look on his face, and Knox filled him in on all that had happened since he had seen him last.

"Well, I'm glad that you're going to do the honorable thing and marry Miss Lila York. That is something," Renford stated, sipping his beer. "I admit I have not seen the elder Miss York for several years, but thinking back to Derby's wedding, the sisters were alike even then." He paused in thought. "No matter how it all came about, Billington, you must feel something for the elder Miss York? The younger cried off and did not want your affections, but the elder does.

Mayhap this farce may end all the better for you. Especially if your wife desires you, that is always welcome in such unions. Or so I have been told." Renford met his eyes over the rim of his glass.

Knox sighed, leaning back in his chair and closing his eyes, wishing everything and everyone would disappear to give himself a moment of peace.

"I have been conned, and now I must marry Miss Lila York."

"Because you were caught alone at the Collins ball? But that is not all, is it? You've been a cad. Admit it," Renford stated.

And because as a gentleman, he could not leave her to face the scandal alone, not after everything else he had done with her. The many times they had been alone and intimate.

His mouth watered at the thought of her, and he ran a frustrated hand through his hair. "Every time I see her, I'm reminded of her betrayal, and I'm mad all over again. But in turn, I also cannot keep my hands to myself."

"That is a problem, an enjoyable one, but a problem nonetheless."

"You are so useful," Knox stated, glaring at his friend.

Renford chuckled, finishing his beer. "How long do you suppose you'll be angry with your betrothed? It will not make for a welcome and harmonious marriage if you're always growling at her."

A fact he knew perfectly well and one he needed to think through. "I think she needs to be punished a little while longer, but I hope in time I may not feel like such a fool for not learning the truth. How could I have not seen a difference? Even the smallest." Knox remembered the moles on the sisters' faces and how they were, in fact, on opposite sides of their mouths. How had he not felt a change? The moment the elder Miss York had returned to town, the emotions she wrought within him were present, strong, and overwhelming. More than he could deny.

How had he not realized?

"The *ton* will eat us alive when they find out, but I have a plan for that particular problem."

"You do?" Renford asked. "What is it?"

"I'll merely state it was Miss Lila York all along and that both ladies were in town unbeknownst to the *ton*."

"And your feelings toward the elder Miss York. You were courting the younger sister but a month ago. Do you have any emotional attachment to her?" Renford threw him a consoling glance. "I merely ask because you're about to marry the eldest, but if you do not love her, no matter the hurt that the elder Miss York will feel, I'm sure she will not want to marry a man who is not emotionally attached."

Renford made a good point, but little did he know Knox was besotted with the woman he was to marry. Loved her, in fact.

Lila was different, more in melody with him, more emotionally available, and passionate. So damn intense that she left him spinning. He'd had not the slightest inkling to kiss the younger Miss York when she had been the one before him. But the elder, well, that was a completely different situation.

The memory of them at his small estate just outside of London... How could that have been but a few days ago? It seemed like so much had happened since. So many twists and turns to his courtship with the woman who would be his wife.

He had all but ruined her reputation. Should the *ton* find out what he had done to her on his small estate, but not just there, the carriage, the theater. She turned him into a rake, and they both enjoyed every scandalous, daring time together because of it.

But she had lied to him.

The one thing that he hated most in people. And she had lied repeatedly to his face. Had made him fall in love with her while letting him believe she was another. Merely to do her sister's bidding and leave him alone and bereft in London when the Season came to an end.

Anger thrummed through him at being

made a fool of, turning the Billington name into the *ton's* latest on dit. He loathed such things and still could not believe that she would be so passionate in his arms and speak such sweet words with such lying lips.

"The elder Miss York and I were caught alone. I cannot marry the younger now, no matter my feelings." Nor had he spent any time between her legs like the elder. A place he wished to visit again, even as angry as he was. "No, the elder Miss York will be my wife, and there is little to be done about it other than ask you if you will stand up with me as my witness. We're to be married at my estate in York."

"Of course," Renford said. "I shall travel with you up north as soon as you're ready to leave. There is nothing keeping me in town."

"Thank you, my friend. We leave next week once her family is in town and the contracts are settled." How that would go was anyone's guess. A disaster all around and of the York sisters' making.

TWENTY-TWO

Lila sat in the private parlor upstairs, her mother and father having long retired to bed. Her sister Harlow stared at her with an annoyance she had never seen on her visage before, and she understood why she was so very mad.

She had every right to be.

"You were sent to London to pretend to be me. To let Lord Billington down with very little fuss and then to come home. How was it that we receive word that you're betrothed to him? What were you thinking, Lila? This is an utter disaster."

Lila moved to sit beside her. She tried to take her hand, but Harlow wrenched away and shuffled further along the settee. "I'm too mad at you right now to allow you to comfort me. How could you do this to me?" Harlow demanded.

Lila sighed, slumping back on the soft cushions. "I'm sorry. I tried to tell him, I really did, but he asked for time to change my mind. I did not think it would hurt and agreed, not knowing that I would fall for his charms by allowing him to court me as he did."

"Oh please, do spare me, Lila. You have always admired Lord Billington, and I should never have trusted you to do what I asked. I should have known you would fall in love with the man."

Lila clasped her hands tight in her lap, hating that her sister was right, no matter how much it hurt to hear her pain. "We must pretend that you were here in London the entire time and that the *ton* was merely confused by that fact. When the time comes that they find out the truth of who Billington has indeed married."

"Perhaps I ought to marry him and save everyone's reputation. They think it is me in any case, and you were only caught together in the Collins library. Nothing untoward has occurred...has it?" Harlow asked, staring at her with such intensity that her body broke out in a cold sweat.

Lila shook her head. "Ah, yes, that is right. We were caught talking and nothing more."

"Well then, the issue will be easy to remedy. I shall marry him."

"No, you will not," Lila stated, her tone brooking no argument. "I have done more than that at other locations with his lordship. I have perchance done more than I'm willing to discuss further. You will not marry him, for I will be doing so." Lila stood, her stomach churning at the thought of her sister being forever tied to the man she had come to adore. No, she could not abide such pain. Her heart would not endure it.

"And anyway, do you not like Lord Kemsley? Do not tell me you have given up already on the earl before trying to win his heart."

"Do you even know the scandal that will ensue when the *ton* finds out that Billington married you instead of me? No matter my feelings on Lord Kemsley, I think it is best for us both and our family and friends that I sacrifice myself and marry his lordship and fix all our concerns."

Lila shook her head. "No, Harlow. I will not allow it. If I do not marry Billington, I know that I will not be happy with anyone else. I've fallen in love with him. As terrible as that sounds, I have. I did not mean to, but he was so very convincing in his praise of me, and I could not be immune to him. I love him," she said again as if by doing so, she too would believe it.

"Except can you be certain he cares for you in return, Lila? He thought he was declaring himself to me, not you. Anything that he has said was for me."

Lila swallowed, hating that her sister was right. But deep in her heart, she had wanted to believe that no matter what he said, he meant it all for the woman before him, which was Lila, not Harlow. Her likes and dislikes were Lila's, not her sister's. Her temperament, her ability to make him laugh, to kiss her with passion, all of those things were from her, not Harlow.

That had to make a difference. Surely he felt the contrast between them.

"Are you trying to hurt me on purpose? Why are you saying such things to me?" Lila asked her sister as trepidation and doubt started to niggle her mind. More so than it had before.

Her sister sighed and took her hand for the first time since she arrived. "I do not mean to say things that will upset you, but I'm concerned, that is all. I do not want you to be hurt."

Lila shrugged, unsure what the best outcome should be, but she knew to her very core that she could not marry anyone else but Billington. And she certainly knew to watch him marry her sister would break her heart where it would never be whole again.

"I will discuss the matter with Billington, but there are things that transpired which I do believe the gentleman within him cannot allow him to choose anyone but me. All will be well, Harlow. We will marry and everything, the gossip and rumors, will settle, and another scandal will take precedence over ours, and all will be forgotten. I promise," Lila said, trying to believe her words, and not just for her sister's benefit.

Harlow's raised disbelieving brow stated otherwise.

KNOX WELCOMED THE YORKS AND A group of close friends from London whom he trusted and knew would help with the scandal that would soon break about London when he married Miss Lila York instead of Harlow.

He had not seen the younger sister, having preferred to keep his distance since she had been the mastermind behind duping him in the first place.

But there was no getting away from her now. Not with her staying at his country estate and soon to be his sister-in-law.

He sat behind his desk and stared at the many ledgers before him. All of them up to date and accurate after a day of hiding away in this room to keep from facing what he must.

His future in-laws and sister-in-law.

A knock sounded on his door, and he bade them entry, expecting it to be Renford, who was expected tonight from London. But instead of his good friend, Miss Harlow York entered, the mole on the opposite side of her face to Lila's giving her away.

He took a calming breath, fighting to keep his annoyance at the chit from coming to the surface. He did not want to make her cry, but the expletives locked away after her trickery severely wanted to come out.

"Lord Billington, may we speak?" Harlow asked, standing beside the door as if she were too afraid to enter farther.

He gestured for her to come in, not bothering to stand. "Have a seat, Miss York," he offered, knowing he was being very ungentlemanly by not holding out a chair, but after what she had done, she did not deserve such manners at this time.

"Thank you," she said, coming to sit before him.

He studied her, unable to see how he had missed the differences between the two sisters. On the surface, yes, they were similar, but not exactly so.

Lila had a mischievous lift to her lips that had always made him smile, where Miss Harlow did not. Notwithstanding the mole location, her hair was not as light as Lila's, and it did not look as if sunlight had kissed her head and left its mark.

"What is it you wished to discuss?" he asked formally.

She settled her skirts, and he saw her hands shake a little from her nerves. "I wanted to talk to you about why I placed my sister in the situation I did, and I need you to know that she did not want to do as I asked."

"Really?" he interrupted. "But she agreed to fool me anyway."

She nodded. "Well, yes, she did, but only because she loves me too much, I fear, and wanted to protect me from myself. I can sometimes get into situations that are not conducive to my own happiness."

"Meaning I placed you in such a situation, that is what you're saying, is it not, Miss York?"

"Well, yes, I suppose I am. I did not feel anything toward you, my lord. Not in the way I want to when being courted by a man. I want to feel butterflies in my stomach and excitement at the thought of seeing my admirer at any ball or party. I want them to occupy my mind at every waking and non-waking hour. I did not feel that way with you," she said rather bluntly.

Knox narrowed his eyes. "Why did you not be honest with me? I'm a grown man. Let me assure you I would have understood."

"But you did not. My sister did answer your offer with a no, and you refused to accept her reply. You created a game where you could try to seduce her into a yes, and then you punish her for it after the fact, when she fell for your charms."

Shame washed through him, knowing Lila's sister was correct in more ways than one. He had coerced Lila into giving him to the end of the Season to seduce her to his doing. And she had fallen at his feet, more than willing to be swept up in his arms.

He should not have done that.

"I understand your point, and I apologize for contradicting myself. I will be sure to make amends with Lila over that fact." But others, he was not so ready to forgive.

"I made her do this to you, my lord. Please do not punish her for falling in love with you when your charms won her heart forever. If you wish to be angry at anyone, be angry at me. I'm the worst of siblings, but I intend to rectify my wrongs, which is why I'm speaking to you today. I'm sorry, I am, and I hope we can be friends."

Knox studied her for a long moment before the anger and embarrassment he held toward both sisters seeped from his heart. Mayhap they had all been wrong in some way or another. Certainly, he should have accepted Miss York's denial of him and left it at that. But he had not. Lila had tried to do the right thing, and he would not let her.

He stood and walked around the desk, holding out his hand, which Miss York took.

He pulled her to stand. "I accept your apology, and I thank you for explaining. I do not have any siblings, so I do not know the level of depth of love you have for one another, but I can understand it enough to know it would be great. You are forgiven," he said, laughing when she wrapped her arms about him and held him fiercely.

"Thank you, my lord. I truly did not mean to cause so much strife. I was too scared to tell you my feelings myself, forcing Lila to do it for me. A cowardly act, I know, but it is the truth."

He hugged her back, glad he would not be at odds with Lila's sister. Such disruptions were not conducive to a happy marriage.

"I forgive you," he said, just as the door opened and Lila skidded to a halt at the threshold. She glanced between them, noticing their arms entwined, and her face blanched.

"Lila," he said, pulling from Harlow's arms and moving toward her, but she was already gone.

He cringed, understanding what it was she believed she had just witnessed. "Blast," he swore before going after her.

Twenty-Three

Knox caught sight of her gown slipping around the staircase railing upstairs as she made her way toward her room. He took the stairs two at a time, not making her door quick enough to stop it from slamming in his face.

He stood there momentarily and took a calming breath before knocking and entering without a by-your-leave.

He found Lila walking out of her dressing room with a small valise in hand. "Pack my things, Eve. I'm leaving today," she ordered, glaring at him before she walked to her bedside cabinet, picking up several books and placing them on the bed. "Oh, and order a carriage too."

"Do not order a carriage," he amended, holding the door open. "Please leave, Eve. I wish to speak to my betrothed alone."

The wide-eyed maid glanced back and forth

between them but did as he bade, hastily exiting the room without another word.

She stopped packing and faced him, her arms crossed defensively over her chest. "Leave. There is nothing I wish to say to you." She mumbled something under her breath that he did not catch.

"Lila, what you saw..."

A book flew past his head, and he stilled. Had she just thrown the book at his head? He gaped at her, unable to believe she had just done what indeed she did before he closed the space between them, towering over her. "You could have hit me," he stated obviously.

"I was trying to. It seems I must practice more. My aim is off." She narrowed her eyes, her breathing heavy.

His heart raced also, but not from fear, from the fact they were alone once more. Betrothed and to be married in the morning.

Not to mention the pesky little truth that he loved her.

"You did not wish to strike out at me. There is no reason to be angry," he said. "You walked in on nothing in the library. Let me assure you."

"Assure me?" she scoffed at his words. "You have been absent, distant since you found out the truth. And while I'm sorry, yet again, and I will be sorry again and again for my part in the game played against you, I will not marry you when it is clear you have feelings for my sister. A truth that I should have accepted a long time ago, but I held on to this false hope that it would not be true. That I could make you see me, the real me, and love me instead. But I was clearly mistaken."

She pushed past him, and he clasped her arm, wrenching her to a stop. "I was angry, Lila. Hurt that while I was trying to win your heart, you were trying to find solutions to the trouble your sister had created. I did not know if anything that happened between us meant anything at all to you. Like it did to me."

She met his gaze, and he cursed the unshed tears in her eyes. "I never loved Harlow. I never felt anything for her when she was in town, but she was the diamond, and everyone thought they ought to marry her. Myself included. But the moment you arrived, something ignited in my soul, and I had to have you. I could not accept the no you so politely bestowed at your sister's behest. I wanted you, Lila York. No one else. Not then, and not now. You know how much I want you and how much I want to tell you again and again how much I love you."

She raised one disbelieving brow, staring down her perfect nose at him. "That is not what appeared to be the truth in the library. You looked quite comfortable in my sister's arms. And you can stay there, for I do not believe you," she stated, raising her chin.

Knox shook his head. "You do believe me, but you're being stubborn. Admit it," he stated, clasping her hips and pulling her against him. "Your sister explained her part in the trick played upon me. Made me see the errors that I should not have made."

"Such as?" she queried, not removing herself from his hold. She was soft and warm under his fingers, and he could smell the scent of jasmine that now always reminded him of her.

"When you turned down my offer the first time, I should have, as a gentleman, accepted your answer. Had I done so, perhaps you would have entered the Season as yourself, your sister along with you, and I would have courted you instead. God knows only you fired my blood and made me want to do every ungentlemanly thing I could think of to you and only you."

"Still, that does not explain why you were holding my sister in your arms just before." Hurt flickered in her eyes, and his heart twisted in his chest.

"Lila, I forgave her, and she was relieved by my offer of friendship. She hugged me in her re-lief. That is all. I do not want Harlow. I want you. It is your soul that calls out to mine. I have never felt anything toward anyone that equals what I feel for you. I would give up my life if it meant that you were safe. You are the woman I love and the only woman I will marry tomorrow."

"And the scandal that will ensue from our marriage. London will feel deceived, and rightfully so, just as you have been. What of all of that?"

Knox clasped her jaw, tipping her face up to his. "I do not care what London says or thinks. So long as we're happy, that is all I care about. The Season is almost over. We do not have to return at all if we choose not to. We can lock ourselves away here and enjoy the early days of our marriage together, alone and without the many eyes watching our every move in town."

HOPE AND RELIEF POURED THROUGH HER like wine, and Lila wrapped her arms around Knox's neck, linking her fingers together to stop him from getting away. "I like the idea of staying here and not returning to London. Not until we have to next year."

He shrugged. "We could travel next Season and not return then either if we do not want to. And by the time we arrive back on English shores, there is bound to be another scandal that is far too delicious for the *ton* to ignore, and we will soon be forgotten. Would you like that, *Mon Coeur*?"

"My heart? So you're no longer going to call me *Mon Amour*?"

He grinned, dipping his head and stealing a kiss. "You will always have my love and heart, Lila."

Lila closed the space between them as an overwhelming weight laid across her shoulders these many weeks lifted. She held him tight, drinking in the scent of sandalwood and something sweet and intoxicating that was all Knox.

"I'm sorry for my part in the scheme against you. I was supposed to tell you no and leave. But I have always harbored affection for you, a gentleman I admired and coveted, even though I knew you did not even know I existed. And when you turned your charms toward me, well, I bathed in them with glee while knowing all along what I was doing was wrong. I was selfish and put myself before you when you knew nothing of the game we played against you."

He met her eye, and she saw no malice there. No anger or resentment.

Just love.

"I forgive you, Lila. How could I not when you are my match in every way? You are my life."

Lila kissed him deeply, took his lips, and conveyed all the emotions that she had so long been fighting with and hiding and lobbed them into the embrace.

He kissed her back, and they toppled onto

the bed. Their legs tangled, his hands were everywhere, stripping her of her gown, and she did not refuse. She, too, was busy working the buttons on his falls, pulling his shirt from his breeches and wrenching off his coat.

Their joining was quick, frenzied, and she gasped when he took her, made her his from this day forward. Their mouths fused, a kaleidoscope of emotions of promises, needs, and wants that had built up over these many weeks.

He thrust into her, taking her with relentless strokes that ignited a fire in her soul that she had never felt before. So much stronger, wilder than when they had been together before. It was nothing like this. This joining was maddening, taunting, fierce, and scalding.

Sweat pooled on her skin, cooling her even though her body was alight with fire. "Knox," she moaned as he continued to take her, pushing her toward the release she craved, one she would always want now that she had tasted the heaven he could gift her.

"I love you so much, Lila," he whispered against her lips, kissing her soundly.

Tears pooled in her eyes just as the exquisite tremor rocked her body, sending her over a cliff of bliss. She held on to Knox, moaned his name, and felt his cock harden further within her.

"Lila," he gasped. "You are everything." He moaned, following her into the pool of ecstasy.

They stayed locked in each other's arms for many minutes, neither one willing to give up the peace and euphoria they had shared.

"I fear I shall never give you respite again. I want you even now," he admitted.

She chuckled, rolling to lay on his chest and stare up at him when he moved to her side. "Do not worry, my love. You shall hear no complaints from me."

He rolled her onto her back, staring down at her with a wicked grin. "Do not say you were not warned, *Mon Coeur*."

"Noted," she said, pulling him down for another kiss. "But please, call me Lila."

Twenty-Four

K nox stood at the altar with Renford at his side. The doors to the small, quaint church opened, and he heard the few mumbling gasps of their friends as Lila entered on her father's arm.

He turned and felt the punch to his gut at the sight of Lila walking toward him. She wore the lightest blue dress of tulle silk, almost white, which made her look ethereal and otherworldly, certainly out of his league.

Her attention was on him, and he could see the love and adoration in her fierce green depths. Their coming together yesterday, the passionate encounter that had turned into many, would forever be the start of their forever.

How lucky he was to be marrying the woman he loved and adored. If only every person were so fortunate. Today was a celebration, the start of something new—a union between them and no one else.

Renford clapped him on the shoulder, and he blinked, flicked a stray tear from his cheek, and hoped no one else saw his emotional response to his future wife.

He reached out and took her hand, wanting her to stand beside him, now and forever.

"We are gathered here today..." the priest began.

Knox smiled, wanting to comfort her. He had been less than what he should have been toward her these past days, but no more. In fact, he had been an utter ass, but never again. She had made a mistake, and he had forgiven her, but he too was not without fault, and he too had a card in the game played against him.

"Lord Billington," he heard the priest say, and gave the man of the cloth his full attention. "Repeat after me."

Knox did as asked and fought back a grin when Lila, too, repeated her vows, her sweet voice like music to his ears. His heart twisted in his chest at the sight of his wife, the woman who held his heart and soul in the palm of her hands, now and forever.

"I now pronounce you husband and wife," he said.

Against the rules of society, Knox pulled his wife close and kissed her, taking her lips in a kiss that would otherwise be only between them. But he wanted everyone to know that Lila York, now Viscountess Billington and future Duchess of Lancaster, was his and that he loved her and only her.

He smiled through the kiss as their friends and family oohed, and several of them clapped.

Knox pulled back, keeping Lila close. "Happy, my love?" he asked her.

"Yes," she nodded. "I'm so happy. I think I could burst from what I'm feeling inside."

"Good, because that's how I intend to make you feel from this day forward until death do us part."

She clasped his cheek, kissing him a second time. "I look forward to it," she said.

As did he.

Epilogue

1812 London

Knox signed the last of the paperwork and bade his solicitor good day before heading for the morning room at the back of the house. He found Lila knitting on a chair in the sunlight, her cheeks still rosy from their morning exertions.

He leaned against the doorframe for a moment, hoping this time maybe they would succeed in producing a child of their own. The last two years of marriage had been wonderful, but he knew that Lila wanted a son or daughter, and it was his life mission to give her everything she wished.

Not that he was complaining. He was more than willing to participate in her bedsport whenever and whatever time she liked.

"I can feel you watching me," she said, grinning down at her knitting. "Are you going to come and join me? You have a scarf to finish, you know."

He grinned, coming into the room and slumping down on the settee beside her, playing with a little ribbon that was embroidered on her gown. "What are you knitting today?" he asked, even though it was clear from the shape of her work what it was she was knitting.

"A baby bonnet." She held it up to him, and he marveled at her neat stitch and how tiny the bonnet was.

"I cannot imagine a baby being so small, but I suppose they are."

"They are," she said, turning to look at him. "What did your solicitor want? I hope everything is well with the estates and farms."

He marveled at her, his perfect viscountess. So caring of others, so much so that he was sure their tenant farmers liked her more than himself these days.

"He came to inform me that my father's distant relative has passed, and we're now the Duke and Duchess of Lancaster and all that it entails."

She dropped her knitting, her mouth agape. Unable to miss an opportunity when one presents itself, he leaned forward and kissed her.

"Do be serious, Knox. Are you certain?" She

frowned, her eyes filling with tears. "How sad that he has passed, and we never came to know him."

Knox pulled her into his arms and rubbed her back, unsure where this emotional response came from toward a man whom they had never met, but it only proved further what a good heart she had. "He did not want us to know him. He was a recluse, remember."

She sniffed and dabbed at her cheeks. "That is true and some consolation, I suppose."

"So tell me, how does it feel to be a duchess?" he asked her, wanting to cheer her up.

She picked up her knitting, shaking her head at his question. "The same as it felt becoming a viscountess. Both are equally frightening and wonderful at the same time. Especially when taking on those titles means I get to be married to you," she said, leaning toward him and bestowing upon him another kiss.

Knox reveled in her touch. "I adore our life, Lila. When I think about what I could have done, what so many men of the *ton* do merely to do their duty and marry anyone at all, I shudder at the thought. I have never been so happy or content. I cherish you," he said.

The blush on her cheeks deepened. "I love you too," she said, packing away her knitting before turning to face him.

"Who is the knitting for? Is Hailey pregnant again?" he asked.

Lila chuckled, shaking her head. "No, it is for our child."

He reached out, taking her hand. "It will happen one day, my love. I believe good comes to good people, and you deserve all that your heart desires."

"I know," she said. "But when I said this is for our child, I meant it." She grinned impishly. "Doctor Riley was here when you were in with your solicitor, and he confirmed my suspicions."

The room spun, and Knox reached out, clasping her arms. "Are you certain?" His mind fought to make sense of her words. "So the sickness you've been experiencing is normal? The dizziness and hot sweats are nothing to be concerned about."

She shook her head, chuckling. "No, nothing to worry about, but I can see you've been secretly worried about me. Why did you not say anything?"

"I did not want to admit to myself that something could be wrong, I suppose."

She sighed, wrapping her arms around his neck. "Well, nothing is wrong, my love, and we'll either have a little lady or a lord in several months."

"Or a duke," he grinned.

She smiled. "Or a duke," she agreed, kissing him again before they partook in more bedsport, even though this time there was no reason for it other than love.

For each other.

Dear Reader,

Thank you for taking the time to read *Surrender to the Duke*! I hope you enjoyed the sixth book in my Wayward Woodvilles series!

I'm forever grateful to my readers, and if you're able, I would appreciate an honest review of *Surrender to the Duke*. As they say, feed an author, leave a review!

Alternatively, you can keep in contact with me by visiting my website, subscribing to my newsletter or following me online. You can contact me at www.tamaragill.com.

Tamara Gill

Don't Miss Tamara's Other Romance Series

The Wayward Yorks

A Wager with a Duke

My Reformed Rogue

Wild, Wild, Duke

The Wayward Woodvilles

A Duke of a Time

On a Wild Duke Chase

Speak of the Duke

Every Duke has a Silver Lining

One Day my Duke Will Come

Surrender to the Duke

My Reckless Earl

Brazen Rogue

The Notorious Lord Sin

Wicked in My Bed

Royal House of Atharia

To Dream of You

A Royal Proposition

Forever My Princess

Only an Earl Will Do

Only a Duke Will Do

Only a Viscount Will Do

Only a Marquess Will Do

Only a Lady Will Do

A Time Traveler's Highland Love

To Conquer a Scot

To Save a Savage Scot

To Win a Highland Scot

A Stolen Season

A Stolen Season

A Stolen Season: Bath

A Stolen Season: London

Scandalous London

A Gentleman's Promise

A Captain's Order

A Marriage Made in Mayfair

High Seas & High Stakes

His Lady Smuggler

Her Gentleman Pirate

A Wallflower's Christmas Wreath

Daughters Of The Gods

Banished

Guardian

Fallen

Stand Alone Books

Defiant Surrender

A Brazen Agreement

To Sin with Scandal

Outlaws

About the Author

Tamara is an Australian author who grew up in an old mining town in country South Australia, where her love of history was founded. So much so, she made her darling husband travel to the UK for their honeymoon, where she dragged him from one historical monument and castle to another.

A mother of three, her two little gentlemen in the making, a future lady (she hopes) keep her busy in the real world, but whenever she gets a moment's peace she loves to write romance novels in an array of genres, including regency, medieval and time travel.